GOLDEN
GOAL

GOLDEN GOAL

David Starr

James Lorimer & Company Ltd., Publishers
Toronto

James Lorimer & Company Ltd., Publishers acknowledges the support
of the Ontario Arts Council (OAC), an agency of the Government of
Ontario, which in 2015-16 funded 1,676 individual artists and 1,125 or-
ganizations in 209 communities across Ontario for a total of $50.5 million.
We acknowledge the support of the Canada Council for the Arts, which
last year invested $153 million to bring the arts to Canadians throughout
the country. This project has been made possible in part by the Government of Canada and with the support of the Ontario Media Development
Corporation.

Cover design: Tyler Cleroux
Cover image: iStock

978-1-4594-1226-2
eBook also available 978-1-4594-1204-0

Cataloguing data available from Library and Archives Canada.

Published by:
James Lorimer & Company Ltd.,
Publishers
117 Peter Street, Suite 304
Toronto, ON, Canada
M5V 0M3
www.lorimer.ca

Distributed by:
Lerner Publisher Services
1251 Washington Ave N
Minneapolis, MN, USA
55401
www.lernerbooks.com

Printed and bound in Canada.
Manufactured by Friesens Corporation in Altona, Manitoba, Canada in
January 2017.
Job #229614

*This book is dedicated to
my wife Sharon, my son Aidan, the Edmonds
Community School Eagles, Canada Scores
Vancouver, Staff Sergeant Major John Buis,
Cst. Aaron Cheng and the Burnaby RCMP,
Jeff Clark of the Burnaby Fire Department and all
those who make a difference in the lives of our youth.
Thank you.*

Contents

Prologue
Dylan's Dream

"Tony! I'm open!" Dylan West shouts, streaking down the middle of the soccer field. It is the final game of the Burnaby School District Championship. The Regent Heights Knights are tied with Fifth Avenue Elementary School, deep in the last minutes of the second half.

"I see you!" cries Tony Delmonico, Regent's other forward. Dylan doesn't even have to call for the ball. After all, he's played soccer with Tony and Emmanuel Gordon, Regent's all-star goalie, since Kindergarten.

Tony leans into the ball, passing it perfectly. The ball bounces once, landing at Dylan's feet. Without slowing down, Dylan takes control of the ball. He dribbles expertly down the field toward the crease. Dylan knows there is only one nervous-looking defender between him and the goal, one Dylan has owned all game.

"Go, son!" Dylan's dad cheers from the sidelines. Dylan smiles. His dad is his biggest fan. He never misses a game, rain, shine or snow. Dylan's dad always comes to his games, even away games like this one.

Ten metres from the goal, Dylan fakes right. The defender falls for it. Dylan drags the ball back to the left, leaving the helpless defender behind him. The goalie approaches, trying to cut off the angle. Dylan darts quickly, taking the goalie off-balance. As the goal opens wide in front of him, Dylan pulls his left foot back.

When he kicks it, the ball takes off like a rocket. It flies through the air toward the top left corner of the goal. The goalie stretches desperately, but he is out of position. There is no way he can reach it in time. The ball hits the back of the net, pushing it out like a balloon. The Regent Heights fans cheer. Dylan's dad is the loudest.

Tony and the rest of the team surround Dylan.

"MVP! MVP!" Tony chants.

This is the best moment of Dylan's life.

"I'm so proud of you, son," his dad says, hugging Dylan tightly. "How do you feel?"

"Like I'm in a dream," Dylan says.

"This is no dream," his father replies. "You worked hard for this. You earned it."

"Thanks, Dad," says Dylan, hugging him back. *If this is a dream, I never want to wake up!*

1
The First Day of School

"Wake up, Dylan! It's time to get ready for school." Dylan groaned at the sound of his mother's voice. He pulled his pillow over his head, his heart still racing. For just a moment, he had been back in his old life. But the good dream was over. It was replaced by the nightmare he was living six months after his father's death.

"Dylan!" His mother was louder this time. "Get out of bed! You don't want to be late for your first day at your new school, do you?"

Dylan groaned again as he crawled out from under the covers. He couldn't care less if he was late for school, or if he never went to school again. It was January. He should be nearly halfway through Grade 7 at Regent Heights. Instead, today was his first day at Grandview Community School. Grandview was a new, terrible school close to their new, terrible apartment in their new, terrible neighbourhood.

"Mom, please," Dylan begged, sitting up. "Let me

take the bus back to Regent. I'm thirteen now. I'm old enough."

"We've had this talk before." Even through the bedroom door Dylan could hear the frustration in his mom's voice. "Regent's too far. You'd have to take the bus to the north side of town. That's forty-five minutes away. And then you'd have to walk two kilometres to the school. Besides, until we get back on our feet I can only afford one Compass Card for transit. And I need it to SkyTrain downtown."

Until we get back on our feet.

Dylan had heard that a thousand times since they moved from Vancouver to the southeast corner of Burnaby. That, and *it's not in our budget*. He hated those expressions. They meant no cell phone, no new shoes or clothes for school, no allowance and no computer.

And they meant no chance of repeating the school district championship at Regent. Dylan wished he was back in his dream, in his old life where the Knights had beat Fifth Avenue Elementary 4–1 and he had scored two goals.

Suddenly the memory of his dad running out onto the field, healthy and full of life, vanished. It was replaced by the horrible image of a hospital bed, his dad thin and bald, connected to machines with wires and tubes. "Don't worry, son," his dad had said, squeezing Dylan's hand. "I'll beat this."

But his dad hadn't beaten the disease. He was gone. Maybe it was a good thing Dylan wasn't playing soccer anymore. He couldn't remember ever playing a game without his dad watching.

Dylan got dressed and stepped out of the only bedroom in the apartment. They'd only been here for two weeks. He still couldn't believe how tiny, how *gross* the place was, even with the Christmas decorations still up.

It had been the worst Christmas ever, just his mom and him in this rotten place. The whole apartment was smaller than the family room in their old house. There were water stains on the ceiling, and the carpet was a terrible browny-orange colour.

Every piece of wood, every appliance was old, faded and ugly. They still had some of their old furniture, and a new sofa-bed his mom had bought for herself. She'd given Dylan the apartment's one small bedroom while she slept in the living room.

Dylan walked from the tiny living room to the even smaller kitchen. He opened the fridge for the milk. As he poured himself a bowl of cereal, he couldn't keep his feelings from showing in his face.

"I don't like it either, honey," his mom said as Dylan sat down to eat. "I didn't want to have to sell the house. But you know we couldn't afford the mortgage. Besides, it won't be forever, you know, just until we…"

"… get back on our feet. I know, Mom," Dylan said. *One thousand and one times*, he thought. "Do I get to eat lunch today at least?" he asked grumpily. "Or do I have to go without food *until we get back on our feet again*?"

"I talked to your new principal, Ms. Bhullar." His mom ignored his sarcasm. "I signed you up for the school lunch program. I saw the menu when I registered you at Grandview before the Christmas break. It looks pretty good."

Dylan was horrified. Everybody knew that the lunch program was for poor kids. "Are you kidding me? Mom, please, an apple or a peanut butter sandwich. I don't need much. I don't want to be on the hot lunch program. Come on, Mom. You're an accountant or something. Are you saying that we can't afford lunch?"

"That's enough, Dylan." His mom's face was red and her eyes bright with tears. "Doing the books for your father's business hardly makes me an accountant. I was lucky to get a job as a payroll clerk. You didn't ask for this, I didn't ask for this and your father certainly didn't ask for this. But now we have to just deal with it. You have a roof over your head and a school to go to, which is more than a lot of people have. So stop complaining."

"Fine." Dylan angrily scooped up his coat and backpack. "You have a nice day being a *payroll clerk*." Fighting back his own tears, Dylan opened the apartment door and slammed it behind him.

As bad as their apartment was, the rest of the building was worse. The carpet in the hallway was stained and ripped, and everything smelled old, musty and stale. He reached the lobby, pushed open the front door and stepped out onto Salisbury Street.

There wasn't one house on Salisbury, just a dozen or so three-storey apartment buildings. Somebody with a bad sense of humour had named all the buildings after trees — Cedar Place, Aspen Glade, Evergreen Gardens. Dylan and his mom lived in Maple Grove.

What stupid names, thought Dylan as he walked up to Grandview Boulevard. The only thing even close to a tree on this street was a large, ugly bush beside Cedar Place.

The buildings weren't the only things named wrong. *Grandview? There's no view at all. Why would anyone name this stupid street Grandview?* He looked up the busy commuter route, full of drivers heading downtown to work. Now, Regent Heights had a view. From Dylan's old bedroom he could see the snow-covered North Shore Mountains, from West Vancouver all the way to Indian Arm. All he saw from his new bedroom was the back of the next building.

Back in Regent Heights almost nobody walked, but here the sidewalks were full. Women wearing scarves over their heads waited for the bus with small children. Dylan watched a man who looked like he was from Africa open the steel shutter on a store that said Halal Meats.

You didn't see things like this on Pinewood Crescent, his old street in Regent Heights. Pinewood was lined with large fir trees, including the one in their backyard. His dad had built him a tree fort in one of them when he was little. He'd played in the fort for hours on end with his best friends Tony and Emmanuel.

But those days were over. Now he had to *just deal with it.* If only it were that easy.

2
Ms. Jorgensen's Class

Lost in his thoughts, Dylan reached Grandview Community School, an old, two-storey, white and green building next to a fire hall.

To get to the school doors, Dylan had to cross the soccer field.

If you can call it a field, he thought. At Regent he'd played on a field of brand new artificial turf. Here, the students kicked their soccer ball on a lumpy gravel playing field. The goals were wooden, and the top bar of one sagged slightly. There was no netting, no crease and no touch line. It was the ugliest soccer field Dylan had ever seen.

The sorry state of their field didn't stop the kids from enjoying their game, Dylan noticed. They chased the soccer ball crazily around the field. Mr. Alvarez, his old coach at Regent, would have blown the whistle right away. *Get your shape! Discipline! Stay in position!*

Dylan almost wanted to laugh. Or maybe cry. Once, soccer had been just about the most important thing in the world to him. But now the game brought back too many painful memories. Dylan never wanted to play soccer again.

Suddenly, the bell rang. Dylan was surrounded by dozens of yelling and laughing children, all anxious to get to class. Dylan thought about just turning around and going home. But then he imagined the trouble he'd get in if he skipped. *I might as well get this over with*, Dylan thought, taking a deep breath. *Like Mom said, I just have to deal with it.*

Dylan was greeted by the principal when he arrived at the school office. "You must be Dylan. Welcome to Grandview Community School," she said, smiling. "I'm Ms. Bhullar."

"Thanks," he said politely. He tried his best to return the smile.

"Your mom told me things haven't been so good for you," Ms. Bhullar said, showing Dylan into her office. "I'll take you to your class in a bit. But I'd like to talk to you a little first."

"Sure." Dylan cringed. The last thing he wanted to do was talk about how awful his life was.

"I'm very sorry for your loss," Ms. Bhullar began. "With your dad's cancer and the move, the last few months can't have been easy."

"It's okay," Dylan said. He wasn't comfortable with starting this way.

Ms. Bhullar nodded. "Some of the kids in this

building have gone through a lot. If you need to talk to somebody, there are lots of adults who can help, including me."

"Sure." Dylan hoped his face wouldn't give away what he was really thinking. *Talk to you? Never in a million years! What do you know about me? You don't understand what I've been through!*

"I mean it, Dylan," Ms. Bhullar went on. "Let me know if you ever need to talk about things."

"Thanks," Dylan said, avoiding eye contact, "but I'm okay."

"Then I guess the next thing to do is get you up to your class. Ms. Jorgensen and your classmates are waiting to meet you."

Dylan followed Ms. Bhullar out of the office. "The intermediate students are upstairs." Ms. Bhullar led Dylan up a wide staircase. "Ms. Jorgensen's class is Division 2. End of the hall, last class on the left. Mr. Briscoe is the other Grade 7 teacher. His class is right next door."

"Dylan! Welcome!" said Ms. Jorgensen as Ms. Bhullar opened the classroom door. "I've got a desk set up for you beside Abbas and Claude." Abbas was an Arabic boy, at least two inches taller than Dylan. Claude was short, slimly built, with dark skin and tightly curled, short-cropped black hair.

"Welcome," Claude said in a French accent as Dylan sat in the empty desk.

"Hey," Dylan replied.

"Hello," Abbas said in formal accented English. "Pleased to meet you."

"You too," Dylan said, taking off his backpack. Every student in the class introduced themselves to Dylan. Then they went back to work.

When Dylan thought about it later, he couldn't remember what Ms. Jorgensen taught that day. All he could recall was sitting beside two strange new boys, thinking about his old life and feeling absolutely, one hundred per cent alone.

"Okay, class," Ms. Jorgensen said, snapping Dylan back to attention. "The bell is going to ring in two minutes. Get your snacks, then go outside and play. But don't wear yourselves out," she added. "We're going to the gym after recess."

When the bell rang the students ran into the hallway.

"Do you have a snack, Dylan?" Ms. Jorgensen asked as Dylan got up. "If not, I have lots of granola bars. The Burnaby Fire Department keeps us well-stocked."

"I'm not hungry," Dylan said. He was, but having to eat the school lunch was bad enough. The last thing his pride could take was a charity snack.

"Okay," his new teacher said. "Then join the rest of the class outside and have fun. You look like you haven't had much of that for a while."

When Dylan reached the playground, most of the boys from Ms. Jorgensen's class were already out on the gravel field, kicking the ball around.

"Do you want to play football — soccer I mean?" Claude asked.

"No thanks," Dylan replied. "I'm just going to hang out."

"Next time then." Claude grinned and ran to join the game.

"Sure. Next time," Dylan said, not meaning it. He sat down on the pavement and leaned against the wall of the school, feeling sorry for himself.

After what seemed like forever, the bell rang. Dylan stood up and slowly made his way back to his classroom.

"Okay, people," Ms. Jorgensen said. "Gym time."

"I hope we get to play basketball," a girl with dark, curly hair said as they walked toward the gym.

"No way! Floor hockey!" a Middle-Eastern boy with black hair and a bright smile replied. "Or volleyball!"

"I have a feeling we'll be playing soccer," said Claude.

"Here we go!" laughed a boy named Jake. "Claude is having another one of his *feelings*. He's like a magician, like Harry Potter or something!"

"Maybe I am." Claude smiled. "I'm also getting a feeling that I'm going to beat you at whatever game we play!"

"Four corner soccer," announced Ms. Jorgensen.

3
The Fight

Not soccer! Dylan groaned to himself as his classmates organized themselves expertly. In less than two minutes the nets were placed in each corner of the gym. They were sorted into four teams wearing different coloured pinnies. Claude was a one, Abbas a three and Dylan a four.

Dylan had played four corner soccer a million times. Each team would wait by their net for the teacher to call out two teams. Those teams would play furiously until the whistle blew and the other two teams took their turn. The winning team was the one with the most goals when the game ended.

"You ready?" called Ms. Jorgensen, putting the ball in the centre of the gym. "Three and four! Go!"

Both teams rushed to get the ball. A girl on Dylan's team, Fatima, was first to touch it. She turned quickly and passed to Dylan. But before he could do anything, Abbas came out of nowhere, stripped him of the ball and fired into the net. Team Three led 1–0.

The Fight

"That was quick!" said Ms. Jorgensen. "Keep playing!"

Jake was on Dylan's team. He took the ball and rushed toward the net. He shot, but the ball went wide, bounced off the wall and came right to Dylan. Dylan moved toward the goal. It was then that Abbas came at him again.

Dylan tried to fake right. But Abbas guessed what Dylan would do and bumped into him. It wasn't hard enough to foul, but enough to take the ball from him again.

"Too slow!" shouted Abbas as he shot, scoring again.

Dylan's cheeks burned. This Abbas kid had embarrassed him twice in two minutes, and now he was rubbing it in. There was no way he'd let it happen again.

The whistle blew. "Three and four back to your corners," said Ms. Jorgensen.

Never taking his eyes from Abbas, Dylan moved off the floor. Dylan watched him smile and goof around with the members of his team. Abbas was making fun of him, he was sure of it. *You won't be smiling soon,* Dylan thought.

It took ten minutes for teams three and four to face each other again. When they did, Dylan did not hang back. Abbas had the ball and Dylan ran at him, hip-checking him roughly. He took the ball and kicked it as hard as he could into the back of the net.

"Hey!" shouted Abbas, rubbing his leg.

"It's not my fault you're too slow," Dylan sneered.

"Take it easy, guys," Ms. Jorgensen warned. "This isn't the World Cup."

Play started again. Fatima took a shot but it was blocked. When the ball rolled into the middle of the gym, Dylan saw Abbas run for it. *No way are you getting that ball*, he thought. The two boys came together, legs kicking furiously trying to gain control. Then Abbas kicked Dylan on the shin. It was the sort of thing that happens when players fight for a ball, but Dylan was furious. He shoved Abbas to the ground.

Suddenly both the ball and the game were forgotten. Abbas jumped to his feet and pushed Dylan hard in the chest. Before he knew it, Dylan was swinging wildly with his fists. Abbas hit back, his fist connecting with Dylan's face so hard Dylan saw stars. Just as Dylan was about to throw another punch, someone grabbed him from behind.

"Claude!" shouted Ms. Jorgensen as she dragged Dylan away from Abbas. "Quick! Get Ms. Bhullar!"

⚽ ⚽ ⚽

Dylan sat outside Ms. Bhullar's office, waiting for his mom. His left eye was swollen shut, and his lip was split. His knuckles were scraped and bleeding. Dylan could see Abbas sitting in Ms. Bhullar's office, nursing similar wounds on his face. Most likely he was telling the principal his side of the story.

The Fight

Dylan didn't care if he was about to be kicked out of school forever. That would be fine, he thought hopefully. He hated Grandview. If Ms. Bhullar expelled him, then his mom would have to let him go back to Regent Heights.

"Dylan!" His mom's face was red and flushed as she hurried into the school office. "You look awful! Do you need to go to the hospital?"

"I'm sure he'll be fine, Mrs. West," said Ms. Bhullar stepping out of her office. "He'll have a black eye. His lip will be swollen for a week or so, but he doesn't need stitches."

"What happened? Who did this to him?" Dylan's mother asked.

"Dylan got into a fight during gym class," Ms. Bhullar said. "And I'm afraid to say that he started it."

"Dylan! You've never been in a fight in your life!" His mom's voice was surprised. But there was something else there too, something he'd never heard before. She was *embarrassed*. She was embarrassed of *him*. Dylan hung his head and shut his eyes.

"Why don't you step into my office and we can talk about it," said Ms. Bhullar. "Abbas," she said over her shoulder, "your mom's coming too. You can wait in the chair in the hallway."

Abbas stood and walked out of Ms. Bhullar's office. He glared at Dylan as he passed. *This isn't over*, his eyes said. Dylan looked away.

He watched Ms. Bhullar and his mom step into the office and close the door. It was then he realized how much his face hurt. Ms. Dawson, the secretary, had given him a plastic bag of ice when he'd first come down to the office. But Dylan had been too angry to use it. He lifted the bag to his swollen lip. Now the bag held nothing but cold water.

"Here's some more ice," Ms. Dawson said, handing Dylan a fresh bag.

"Thanks," Dylan replied. He took the ice gratefully. The cold made his face feel a little better.

Ten minutes later, his mom and Ms. Bhullar stepped out of the office.

"Thank you so much, Ms. Bhullar," his mom said. "Once again, I'm so sorry. Like I said, Dylan's never been in a fight in his life."

"These things happen," the principal said. Then she turned to Dylan. "People make mistakes, Dylan, but you have to learn from them. When you get back to school you will have to fix things with Abbas."

"Yes, Ms. Bhullar," he mumbled. *Get back to school? No way! I'm never coming back here!*

4
Sent Home

As he followed his mom out of the school office, Dylan saw Abbas sitting in the hallway. A woman wearing a scarf that covered her head sat beside him. She touched the cut on Abbas's cheek. She spoke rapidly to Abbas in a language Dylan didn't recognize.

"I'm sorry this happened to you," Dylan's mom said to Abbas. "Dylan's not usually like this — he's been through a lot recently."

Abbas's mom spoke to her son. He shook his head and said something that sounded to Dylan like '*la*'. "I told you to say sorry to that boy," Abbas's mom said slowly, this time speaking in English.

"I'm sorry," Abbas said to Dylan. The look on his face showed that he didn't really mean it.

Abbas's mom extended her arm. "My name is Amira. Amira Wassef," she said.

Dylan's mom took her hand. "Erin West," she said. "I am so sorry for what happened, Mrs. Wassef. Dylan is too. Aren't you?"

"Sorry," Dylan mumbled. He didn't mean it either.

Sincere or not, the apologies were made. There was nothing left to say. Dylan and his mom left the school and walked back to their apartment on Salisbury in silence. It wasn't until they stepped into their place that he finally spoke.

"I hate that school, Mom. Please, I just want to go back to Regent Heights."

His mom looked exhausted. "I can't believe you're still talking about that! Is that why you got into a fight? To go back to Regent?"

"Mom! You don't get it!" Dylan shouted.

"I don't get it, Dylan? I get it perfectly. I had to leave work to get you. Now I'm losing half a day's pay. This is only my second week, for goodness sake! It's you who doesn't seem to get it!"

Dylan lost all control. "I hate you!" he screamed.

"Dylan! Keep it down," his mother said. "Do you want our neighbours to hear you?"

"I don't care!" Dylan was crying now, sobs shaking his entire body. "I hate this apartment. I hate Grandview and I hate Dad for dying and leaving us like this! It's his fault this happened!"

"Dylan!" his mom gasped, but Dylan was beyond caring. He stormed to his room, slammed the door and threw himself down onto his bed.

⚽ ⚽ ⚽

"Dinner's in the fridge," his mom said when Dylan finally came out of the bedroom.

"I'm not hungry," Dylan said. "I don't think I could eat even if I was." His lower lip was swollen, with an ugly red scab where it had split. There was a large yellow and black bruise around his eye. "I'm sorry, Mom," Dylan went on. "I didn't mean all those things — especially what I said about Dad."

Dylan had spent most of the day in his room and had plenty of time to calm down and think about things. He felt awful about how he'd reacted, both at school and at home. He knew his dad wouldn't have wanted him to act that way. His mom had every reason to be embarrassed. Dylan was embarrassed with himself.

"It's okay, honey," said his mom. She put down the book she'd been reading and hugged Dylan. "Things have been very hard for you. We will find a way to get through it."

"How long do I have to stay home?" he asked. Dylan knew that being suspended was the usual punishment for fighting at school. In Grade 6, his friend Tony had gotten into a fight on the playground when a game of tag got out of hand. Mr. Cornell, Regent's principal, had sent him home for three days.

"You're not staying home," his mom replied.

"What? But I got into a fight!" Dylan was shocked.

"Ms. Bhullar said she would prefer to solve things

at the school. That was one of the things we talked about in her office."

"So I'm going back to class tomorrow?"

"You are going back to school tomorrow. But not to your class. You're going to serve a one-day, in-school suspension in the office with Ms. Bhullar tomorrow. And then you're going to make things right with that Abbas boy."

"That's it?" Dylan couldn't believe it. Mr. Cornell would never have gone so easy on a student who got into a fight.

"Not quite," his mom said. "There's something else we agreed you'd do as well."

"What?" Dylan asked nervously. "Detention every day until I'm nineteen or something?"

His mom smiled mysteriously. "You'll have to wait until tomorrow to find that out."

Dylan hardly slept all night. He was worrying about the next day at school. In the morning he left home without eating breakfast. He walked slowly through the January rain and reached Grandview just as the bell rang.

Abbas was waiting in the office. He said nothing as Dylan sat down in the empty chair next to him. Dylan could hardly look at Abbas and the large, ugly bruise on his cheek. Thankfully he only sat for a few seconds before Ms. Bhullar waved them both into her office.

"So, are you two ready to fix this problem?" she asked.

"It was my fault, Ms. Bhullar," Dylan said quickly.

He had made this mess and he wanted to fix it. "Abbas didn't do anything wrong. Abbas kicked me in the leg by accident and I lost my temper." He turned to the boy next to him. "I'm really sorry, Abbas. I didn't mean to hit you." Dylan held out his hand.

"I accept your apology," Abbas said. He shook Dylan's hand, though the look on his face clearly showed he was still angry. Dylan was a little surprised that Abbas was still mad. After all, Dylan had said it was his fault.

"Are you both okay? Really?" asked Ms. Bhullar, eyeing them closely. "Grandview's a small school. And since you two are in the same class, you won't be able to avoid each other. The next time I will have no choice but to send you both home for three days at least. Do I make myself clear?"

"Yes, Ms. Bhullar," the boys said at the same time.

"Good. Abbas, you can go back to class. Tell Ms. Jorgensen I will come and talk to her in a bit. Dylan, you get to work with me today down here."

"You did a good job," the principal said to Dylan when they were alone. "You owned up to your mistake and tried to make it better."

"My dad taught me to do the right thing," Dylan told her.

His dad would have been so disappointed in him for fighting. For what seemed like the millionth time, Dylan fought back the urge to cry.

"Ms. Jorgensen gave me some work for you," said Ms. Bhullar. "I know Abbas said he was fine, but I can tell he's still quite upset. I think you're going to have to come up with a plan to make sure things are truly fixed."

"I know," Dylan said.

"I have an idea if you're stuck," Ms. Bhullar said. "I'll talk to you about it at the end of the day."

5
An Unexpected Consequence

For the rest of the morning Dylan worked at the small table in Ms. Bhullar's office. Wondering what his mom and Ms. Bhullar were hinting at was driving him crazy. He tried to forget about it and do his work. At least Dylan liked the novel Ms. Jorgensen had assigned him to read. He read several chapters and wrote a journal response before he went outside for a break.

Dylan turned his thoughts to Abbas, trying to think of a way to make things up to him. But when he couldn't think of anything, he gave up and turned to math worksheets until Ms. Bhullar told him it was time for lunch.

"It's teriyaki chicken today. It's one of my favourite items on the menu," she said.

"You eat the hot lunch?" Dylan said in surprise.

"Almost every day. I usually eat with the students in one of the classrooms. My favourite place is the kindergarten room. But Ms. Jorgensen's class is pretty fun, too."

Dylan tried to picture straight-laced Mr. Cornell sitting in one of the tiny chairs in the kindergarten room, eating with a bunch of screaming six year olds. It was too much to imagine.

"The butter chicken is good and I like the macaroni and cheese as well," Ms. Bhullar went on. "But once a month, they serve something called a *fun bun*. Don't let Ms. Pucci in the cafeteria fool you. It's nothing but a cheese sandwich. Not very fun at all."

"Where are you going to eat today?" Dylan asked.

"Today you are my special guest. I am going to eat with you," the principal said. "Then after lunch we'll both get back to work."

Together they walked to the cafeteria. Each of them received a tray full of rice and teriyaki chicken, as well as some carrots and milk.

Ms. Pucci looked a little like a bun herself, Dylan thought. She was short and round and kind-looking. Her thick, black hair was covered by a hairnet. "Enjoy your lunch, Dylan," she said as he took his food.

"You know my name?" Dylan was surprised.

"The lunch lady knows everyone." She smiled. "Welcome to Grandview. It's a good school. I think you will like it."

Dylan took the meal back to Ms. Bhullar's office and had a bite. It was good. Really good.

"Your mom said you weren't happy to be signed up for the lunch program," said Ms. Bhullar. "What do you think of the food now?"

"It's okay," Dylan admitted. He wolfed down his lunch. Between his nerves and his sore lip he'd not had much to eat for nearly a full day.

"I'm glad you like it," she said. "Can you tell me why you didn't want to be on the hot lunch program?"

Dylan struggled to answer the question. "When I was at Regent I thought schools with a hot lunch program were for…"

"For poor kids right?"

"I guess so," Dylan murmured. He hoped his answer didn't make him seem like a jerk.

"The students in this school are just as smart and talented as kids in any other school in the city," Ms. Bhullar said. "But a lot of them don't have the same advantages. Some are immigrants, some are refugees. And some are people from right here in Burnaby. We want all of our students to succeed. Success comes easier with a good meal."

After lunch, Dylan took both of their trays back to the cafeteria. Then he returned to Ms. Bhullar's office and went back to work. He read three more chapters of the book, did a vocabulary crossword and completed a map of Renaissance Italy. By the time he was done with the map it was almost three.

"You did well today, Dylan," said Ms. Bhullar. She'd been out of her office most of the afternoon and returned just before the bell rang.

"Do I go back to class tomorrow?" Dylan asked.

"You do," she replied. "As long as you can fix things with Abbas. I don't want you guys back down here after another fight. Have you come up with anything?"

"I'm still thinking," Dylan admitted.

"Well, your mother and I have an idea." Ms. Bhullar grinned. "Did she tell you?"

"No," Dylan said. This was it. He was finally going to learn what his mother had been so mysterious about. "She told me you talked about something with her, but I would have to wait to hear it from you."

"The best way to get to know a person, to understand them, is to spend time with them doing things you like to do. Your mom and I agreed that you need to get back to soccer. Abbas is on the school soccer team, and, as of right now, so are you. We get to kill two birds with one stone, as the old saying goes. The coach has already been told. He's expecting you on the field in fifteen minutes!"

Oh, no! The last thing Dylan wanted was to play soccer. He had to play soccer for Grandview *with Abbas?* He couldn't believe it. Dylan walked slowly onto the field toward the group of boys standing around the goal post.

Dylan saw some of the boys from his class on the field, as well as other kids he didn't know. Claude was there, and he smiled when he saw Dylan. Abbas, on the other hand, glared as he got closer. *Ms. Bhullar must be crazy*, Dylan thought. There was no way playing soccer together was going to fix this. It was soccer that had caused the problem in the first place.

6
Coach T

"All right, guys, do a lap and warm up." The voice came from behind Dylan.

He turned to see a tall man with short, black hair carrying a mesh bag full of soccer balls. *He must be the coach,* Dylan thought, though he didn't much look like one. All of Dylan's coaches at Regent wore team jackets and track pants. This man was dressed in blue jeans and wore a brown leather jacket.

The rest of the team started to jog around the field. Dylan followed slowly behind them.

"Warming up means running, not walking, Dylan West," the coach said, to Dylan's surprise. How on earth did he know his name? Did everyone at Grandview know about him already?

Dylan picked up the pace. He was a good runner, though he'd not had much practice over the last few months. Even in jeans he managed to catch up with the slower players. Abbas was only ten metres ahead. Dylan sped up to close the distance between them.

Soon, Dylan was only a few metres behind Abbas, and gaining quickly.

Abbas turned his head and Dylan knew what that look meant. *You're not going to catch me.*

Oh, yes I am, thought Dylan. The race was on. Dylan forgot about the coach, forgot about soccer, forgot about everything except passing Abbas. Within a few seconds, Abbas and Dylan were sprinting well ahead of the rest of the team. At the corner of the field Abbas turned and entered the home stretch.

With less than fifty metres to go, Dylan was only a few steps behind. He could hear the sound of Abbas's shoes kicking up gravel and of Abbas panting. *He's out of breath*, Dylan thought. *I'm going to beat him.*

Dylan pressed on. With thirty metres to go he was half a step behind. At twenty he pulled even.

Ten metres from the coach and Dylan was about to pass. But Abbas kicked it into high gear. He stretched out his legs and shot forward, almost like he was flying. There was no way Dylan could catch up.

Abbas stopped by the coach and waited for Dylan to arrive. A triumphant smile shone on his face.

"Well done, boys," the coach laughed. "Though I said warm up, not set a new Olympic record for 400 metres! Gather 'round," he said to the rest of the team. "Let's get the season started."

The boys huddled up beside the coach. Some gave him high fives, while a couple even gave him a hug.

"For those who don't know me," said the coach, "my name is Constable Tyrell Whitebear. I'm a School Liaison Officer with the Burnaby RCMP. More importantly, I'm the coach of the Grandview boys' soccer team."

"Go Eagles! Yay, Coach T!" yelled somebody.

"That's right." Constable Whitebear grinned. "You can all call me Coach T. Practices this year will be Tuesdays and Thursdays after school, and games will be every Monday. The schedule's not quite set yet, but our first game will be next Monday. I'll let you know who we play at Thursday's practice. It's going to be a good season."

"We'll make the playoffs for sure!" said Claude. "Maybe even win the championships. I have a feeling."

Claude may have been right before with his 'feelings', but Dylan doubted that Grandview would win a single game. They had no chance at the playoffs. Of the forty elementary schools in the district, only the top eight made the playoffs. Those eight were the best schools, Dylan knew. Schools like Regent Heights.

This would have been Dylan's third year of school soccer at Regent. They'd won last year at Fifth Avenue. The year before they had come in second, losing to Lakewood by just one goal.

"Dylan," said Coach T. "You don't seem to share Claude's confidence."

"No — yes, I'm sure we'll do fine," Dylan said. He stumbled over his words, his cheeks burning.

"To have a successful season we'll have to play good soccer, of course. But more importantly, we'll have to believe in ourselves and each other. We will all have to play as a team, to work together, to trust each other, to care for each other. If we do that, it won't matter to me if we make the playoffs. We'll have done something far more important than winning a trophy."

Dylan could hardly believe his ears. What kind of coach said stuff like that? *It doesn't matter if we make the playoffs? We have to care for each other?* No wonder these losers never won anything. Claude was crazy to think this team had a chance.

"Right," said Coach T, opening the mesh bag. "Let's get started. Take a ball and get loosened up."

Dylan watched Abbas lift his ball off the ground with the top of his foot. He bounced it on his right foot half a dozen times, then changed to his left. He juggled with his knees, and then raised it high with a nifty kick. When the ball was still in the air, Abbas smacked it hard with his left foot, sending the ball cleanly into the net.

"Well done, Abbas," said Coach T. "I see you've been practising."

Abbas looked at Dylan. *Let's see you do better.*

No problem, Dylan thought, flipping his own ball off the ground. He bounced it from foot to foot, knee to knee a dozen times, as easily as if he were walking to school. The other players stopped what they were doing. Word of the fight between Abbas and Dylan had spread across the school like wildfire. Everyone knew what this was really about.

With the entire team watching, Dylan kicked the ball high into the air. He lowered his head and caught it on the back of his neck between his shoulders. It was a trick he'd practised with Tony and Emmanuel for hours. Then, with the Grandview team cheering him on, Dylan quickly flipped the ball back over his head, and blasted it between the goalposts. Dylan smiled. Abbas looked like he was sucking on a lemon.

"Not bad," said Coach T. "Not bad at all. I think we are going to have a very interesting season with you two on the team!"

7
The Scrimmage

Thursday was a perfect day for soccer. The winter sky was empty of clouds. It was cool but not cold, and the gravel field was dry for once. In the middle of drills, Dylan watched Abbas dribble the ball through a line of red cones. Abbas was fast, but he never lost control. It was like the ball was attached to his foot with a string.

After the dribbling drill, Coach T set up the portable nets. No matter how many times he kicked the ball, Abbas never missed. When it was Dylan's turn, he concentrated as hard as he could on his own shot. There was no way he would let Abbas show him up.

"Okay, guys," Coach T said when the drills were done. "Let's play a little game. Six on six. Abbas, Claude, Dylan, Abdul, Mo and Jake on one team. The rest of you on the other. We'll play half field." Jake was a Filipino boy in Dylan's class and Mo was one of several boys from Afghanistan in the school. Abbas didn't seem happy to be playing with Dylan.

Claude, on the other hand, seemed very pleased. "I

have a feeling we're going to win for sure," he beamed. "You two are the best players on the team."

There were no goalies for the scrimmage. Coach T set up the nets and when the players were in position, he blew his whistle. "This is just practice but play hard," he told them. "I want to see some energy out there."

Claude started with the ball, playing midfield. Mo and Jake slid back to defend. Abbas and Dylan played forward, Dylan on the left and Abbas on the right. Both boys sprinted down the field as Claude moved slowly up the centre. Dylan watched as Abbas stutter-stepped, faked out the defender, and raced to an open spot on the field.

Claude lifted the ball into the air. The kick was perfect, landing at Abbas's feet. Without breaking his stride, Abbas took the ball and sprinted toward the small goal.

The defenders, Steven and Jun, moved quickly to cut him off. Abbas was good, but there was no way he could deke out both of them. But both defenders on Abbas meant Dylan was open. Using a clever back heel, Abbas flicked Dylan the ball. With no defenders to worry about, Dylan raced toward the goal and kicked the ball at the small target. The ball rolled into the net. His team erupted in cheers.

"That was a good pass, Abbas," said Dylan. It was the first time he'd actually spoken to Abbas since Tuesday morning in Ms. Bhullar's office. Dylan didn't like Abbas, but he was an awesome soccer player. The pass had been beautiful. It would be poor sportsmanship not to thank him, and Dylan's dad had taught him to be a good sport.

Abbas's face broke into a surprised grin. "The goal was okay too."

The scrimmage continued. Claude was an excellent midfielder, Dylan realized, with a gift for making amazing passes. Like a quarterback throwing the ball to receivers, Claude took charge of the offence. He passed the ball equally to Dylan and Abbas. Dylan and Abbas might not have liked each other, but that didn't stop them from playing very well together.

Not like how it was with Tony, Dylan told himself. After all, he'd played with his best friend since Kindergarten. But Dylan had to admit that Claude, Abbas and he had something his old coach at Regent would have called *chemistry*.

When Coach T ended the scrimmage, Dylan's team was up 7–2. Dylan and Abbas had three goals each, with Claude picking up the other one.

"That was great!" Claude said as they hustled toward their coach.

It was, Dylan had to agree. He was sweaty, tired and thirsty, but felt better than he had for weeks.

"Gather 'round everyone," said Coach T. "I have our schedule. We play eight games in the regular season," he said looking at a sheet of paper. "Six at home and two away. Our first game is next Monday against Griffith Park at their school."

"Griffith Park's only a fifteen minute walk from here," Claude told Dylan. "That's good."

Dylan was confused. He was used to each team playing half their games at home and the rest at another school. It was nice to have so many home games, but it sounded a bit unfair. "Why do we get to play so many home games?" he asked.

"I asked the coaches at Brentford and University Hill if they were okay coming here instead of us trying to go there," Coach T explained. "They said it wasn't a problem."

"Most of our parents don't have cars. And it's too hard for us to get to schools that are far away," explained Jake.

"Oh," said Dylan. He hadn't thought of that. Since moving to Grandview his mom had sold their car — as well as most of their other things.

"Who do we play after Griffith Park, Coach T?" Mo asked.

When Coach T answered, he looked directly at Dylan. "Our second game of the season is against a school from the north side called Regent Heights. I think you may have heard of them. They won the championship last year. Normally we would stick to the south side, but I like our chances this year and I wanted to see how we match up against the best team in the district."

The Scrimmage

⚽ ⚽ ⚽

Within days of starting at Grandview, Dylan realized that he had friends there. Claude was great. And Dylan liked Jake, who was also a great soccer player. Jake was small, but he could dart around the field, sticking his legs out like a striking snake and steal the ball from an attacker.

Mo was funny, even-tempered and, like Abdul, from Afghanistan. Steven was a First Nations kid from Vancouver Island. Jun was Korean, and William and Alvin were twin brothers from Taiwan.

Their goalie, Michael, a tall, red-headed boy, was born and raised in Vancouver like Dylan. Junior was from Liberia, Carlos from El Salvador. Abbas, Dylan learned, was from Syria. But Dylan didn't know how long Abbas had been in Canada, or much of anything about him for that matter — none of the boys did.

Abbas wasn't exactly a friend, though things had been much better between them. They didn't speak to each other often, but at least they hadn't fought again. Both still had bruises on their faces from the fight, but they were fading, as were the bad feelings.

Maybe his mother and Ms. Bhullar had been right after all. Dylan actually looked forward to the feel of the ball against his feet. It felt good to play, but what was even better was making friends. He hadn't realized just how lonely he'd been.

8
The Mall

"Regent was your old school wasn't it?" asked Claude. The boys were eating their lunch in Ms. Jorgensen's classroom. Today Ms. Pucci had served them mac and cheese.

"Yeah," said Dylan. "I went to Regent Heights since Kindergarten."

"How come you moved to Grandview?" asked Mo. "Regent Heights is pretty fancy I hear."

"My dad died. We couldn't afford to stay in our old house so we had to move." Dylan hadn't told anyone how he'd ended up at Grandview. He hadn't planned on telling anyone either, but it just slipped out. Dylan hoped the guys wouldn't ask any more questions.

"My dad's dead, too," said Mo. "I don't really remember him. He died in the war back in Kabul when I was just a baby. We moved to Canada when I was five."

"My dad's in the Philippines," said Jake. "My mom was a nurse back there, but she works as a caregiver here. We're trying to save money to bring him here."

"What about you, Claude?" Dylan asked, glad the guys were no longer asking him questions. "How did you come to Grandview?"

"It's not really that interesting," said Claude, quiet for once.

"Are you crazy?" said Junior. "They should make a movie about you!" Claude blushed at the comment.

"No, really, I'd like to hear it," said Dylan, "but only if you want to." He understood how difficult it was to talk about losing someone you loved.

"I grew up in Congo, in a place called North Kivu," Claude began. "There was a war. One day when I was six and my sister was fifteen, soldiers came to my village. My mother and father told us to hide in the forest. We didn't want to leave them, but we obeyed. We heard shooting and screaming and then we saw a fire. We waited a few hours for the soldiers to leave and then went back to our house."

"What did you see?" Dylan asked. All the boys were listening intently.

"Our house was burned down and my parents were dead," Claude said. "There was no way we could stay in our village, so my sister and I left. We walked for weeks, hiding from soldiers. We crossed the border into Tanzania and we were taken to a refugee camp."

"Refugee camp? What's that?" Dylan felt awful for his new friend. Claude was so happy and cheerful, Dylan couldn't imagine such terrible things happening to him.

"It's a place where people who have fled their country go," said Claude. "It's like a city of tents, run by the United Nations. There wasn't much to do there. There wasn't a school. So I pretty much just played soccer. Sometimes aid workers would give us balls. Other times we would make our own out of rags and string.

"We lived there for three years until we came to Canada," Claude continued. "I registered at Grandview. My sister finished high school, and then she went to college. She's studying to be a nurse and works part time."

"I'm going outside," said Abbas suddenly. He quickly got up from the table and left.

"What's his story?" Dylan asked. He wondered what could have made Abbas so upset. Was it Claude talking about refugee camps?

Mo shrugged. "Abbas came here last spring from Syria. He doesn't like to talk about it. But whatever happened to him before he came to Grandview must have been pretty bad."

⚽ ⚽ ⚽

Dylan quickly forgot about Abbas when his mom got home from work.

"Get your coat on, Dylan," she said. "We're going to Metro Mall."

The Mall

"Really?" Dylan loved Metro Mall. The largest shopping mall in Metro Vancouver had Supersports and Electro Video Games, his two favourite stores in the world.

"I got paid today," his mom said, "and you need some new clothes and a pair of shoes. I can't believe how much you've grown recently."

It was true. For a while now Dylan had felt like everything he owned was shrinking. But he hadn't said anything to his mom, because he knew they didn't have much money. "Are you sure, Mom? I can get by with what I have for another couple of months."

"It's fine, son," his mom said. "I've been putting a little money aside. I can afford to get you some new clothes. We'll do some shopping, and then we can go to the food court for dinner."

"Thanks, Mom, that's a great idea." They hadn't eaten out for so long that even mall food sounded like a treat to Dylan.

They walked out of their small apartment, and instead of turning left on Salisbury, Dylan and his mom went toward the Grandview SkyTrain station. Fifteen minutes later they were on the train, heading the three stops west to the mall.

"Go and have a look around," his mom said at the mall entrance. "There are a few things I need myself and I don't think you want to come with me to buy women's clothes. We'll meet back here, get your things and then eat. I feel like Chinese food!"

There was no doubt where Dylan was going first. There were plenty of stores in the mall where he could buy pants and shirts for school. But only one had what seemed to Dylan like the world's largest collection of jerseys, ball caps and sports-themed items. Supersports was on the second floor of the mall, so Dylan raced to the escalator. Most likely his mom wouldn't buy him anything from Supersports. Team jerseys were expensive, but there might be something on sale left over from Boxing Day they could afford.

Dylan walked into Supersports, looking at the framed and signed Whitecaps, Canucks and Lions jerseys on display. He walked past the shelves of fun stuff, like team piggy-banks and bobble-heads of famous players. Dylan grinned when he saw the clearance rack. The prices were great and Dylan was pretty sure he could talk his mom into getting him something, if only a T-shirt.

Suddenly Dylan heard a voice he knew. There, by a rack of hockey jerseys, were two very familiar faces.

9
Old Friends

"Tony! Emmanuel!" Dylan called, running over to his old friends. It had been more than a month since he'd last seen them, or even heard from them.

"Dylan. Hey," Tony said in surprise.

"How's it going?" Emmanuel asked. "How's the new school?"

"It's okay," Dylan said, "but I sure miss Regent and you guys. When are you going to come and visit? You said you would. But I guess you've been busy."

"Yeah," said Tony. "We went up to our place in Whistler over Christmas. We just got back the day before school started."

"That's great," said Dylan. He'd been with Tony to the Whistler house a few times before his dad got sick. He loved it up there. "What about you, Emmanuel? You do anything fun?"

"We went to Mexico for a week," Emmanuel said.

Dylan felt just the slightest touch of envy, wishing he'd had a fun vacation as well. "You guys want to hang out tomorrow?" he asked.

Tony shifted uncomfortably while Emmanuel looked down at his feet, silent. "I don't think we're allowed to come visit you," Tony finally said. "My mom said your new place isn't in the greatest part of town. She says it isn't very safe."

Tony's words stung Dylan. Sure, Grandview wasn't as expensive as Regent Heights, and his apartment wasn't the greatest. But Tony and Emmanuel had been his friends and teammates for years, and that sort of stuff shouldn't matter.

"Why don't I come over to your place, then?" Dylan asked. "We could play video games or whatever you want to do. I'm playing soccer for Grandview, too. Maybe we could kick a ball around. We're playing each other soon."

"Sorry," said Emmanuel. "I have family stuff to do this weekend."

Then Dylan remembered. "It's your birthday to-morrow, isn't it? I almost forgot." Emmanuel's birthday parties were the highlight of the year. His family always did amazing things to celebrate the event. "Remember last year? Your parents took us snowboarding at Grouse Mountain? That was even more fun than when we went rock climbing for your tenth birthday!"

"Yeah, but we're not really doing much this year," Emmanuel said awkwardly.

"Hey, you guys! Check this out!" Alex, another boy Dylan knew from Regent, suddenly appeared, a soccer jersey in his hands. "It's only 150 dollars! But I won't wear it for your birthday party, Manny. I wouldn't want it wrecked. Paintball and pizza! It's gonna be so fun! Oh, hey, Dylan," Alex added, seeing him for the first time. "How's the new school?"

Then Dylan knew. His friends were lying to him. Emmanuel was going to have an awesome birthday this year after all. But Dylan hadn't been invited.

"Dylan," Emmanuel stammered, his face bright red. "Yes, I'm having a party. I didn't want to tell you because I didn't want to hurt your feelings. I wanted to invite you, but you don't have a phone anymore. I would have left a message on Facebook, but I didn't think you had a computer. I'd ask you now," he said quickly, "but there's a limit on the number of people who can play and…"

"That's cool. I get it. No big deal," Dylan said quickly. "I just remembered I have plans tomorrow anyway." Dylan wanted to run away as fast as he could. His old friends from Regent seemed to feel the same. Tony couldn't even look at Dylan. Alex, who had missed the start of the conversation, seemed confused.

"My mom's waiting for me," said Emmanuel, making a show of looking at his phone. "See you when we play your school."

"I'll message you," said Tony as he, Emmanuel and Alex left the store.

"Sure. Later." But Dylan knew there would be no message from Tony, or from anyone. After all, Dylan didn't have a phone.

Dylan couldn't believe it. He had been out of Regent Heights barely a month and Tony and Emmanuel had already forgotten about him. He may as well have moved to Mars.

In a daze, Dylan walked back to the mall entrance. The happiness he had felt when he arrived had drained right out of him. He barely noticed his mom's approach.

"Hey, Dylan, I'm starving! Are you ready to get some..." She looked at Dylan's face and stopped mid-sentence. "Honey? Are you okay?"

The last thing Dylan wanted to do was tell his mom what happened. She'd been through enough already. She didn't need this.

"I don't feel good. I think I'm coming down with something," he said, thoughts of dinner and new clothes completely gone. "I'm not hungry anymore. Can we please just go home?"

⚽ ⚽ ⚽

Sometime between Friday evening and Monday morning, Dylan's sadness was replaced by anger. Red hot anger. Betrayed. That was the word. Dylan's two best friends in the world had turned against him, thrown him away like a piece of trash. What should have been the best weekend he'd had since his dad died had become the worst.

"Come on, Dylan," his mother said from behind

the bedroom door. "I know you're still not feeling well but you need to get to school. You have a game today, remember? The first with your new team."

And that was another thing. Dylan had somehow fooled himself into thinking things were getting back to normal. That he had soccer and friends and a life. But when he saw how wrong he was, his desire to play soccer had vanished.

"Can't I stay home?" he begged. "Please?"

"No, and that's the final word." The tone of his mom's voice matched her words. End of discussion.

Dylan walked so slowly to school he was almost late. Arriving in Ms. Jorgensen's class when the bell rang, he muttered something to Claude, who greeted him with his usual smile. Then he slumped down into his desk.

Dylan didn't play soccer with the team at recess or at lunch. He told the guys that he was getting over being sick, and didn't want to waste his energy before the game at Griffith Park.

The afternoon passed slowly for Dylan. The other team members in his class could barely control their excitement. But it was all Dylan could do to control his temper. The more he thought about how Emmanuel and Tony had treated him, the angrier he got.

"Dylan," Claude said as the bell rang. "You don't look so good."

"I'm fine," snapped Dylan. They silently walked down to the front door of the school to meet Coach T.

"Here are your uniforms, boys," said the coach, a big duffel bag in his hands. "I've assigned you each a jersey and pair of shorts. Look after them. They're all we have."

Coach T gave Dylan his uniform. The dark green jersey had a golden eagle on the front and the number eight on the back. When Dylan was a Regent Heights Knight, he wore blue and silver and the number seventeen. He thought of his former friends and his anger started to bubble again.

"Are you okay, Dylan?" Coach T asked, eyeing him sharply. "Is it the shorts? Are they too small?"

Why is everyone asking me if I'm okay? Why can't they just leave me alone? Dylan thought. "They'll fit just fine," he managed to say.

"Great," said Coach T. "Get changed and wear them under your clothes for the walk to Griffith Park. It's a little chilly outside and it might rain."

The boys got changed and followed Coach T out of the school. Griffith Park Elementary School was by Grandview SkyTrain Station, twenty minutes away. The boys chatted and joked with each other as they walked — all but Dylan.

"Coach T, is it true you used to be one of those SWAT guys?" asked William. "With the machine guns and the black masks? That sounds so cool!"

"In the RCMP it's called an Emergency Response Team, not SWAT." Coach T grinned. "And it does sound cool. But I wasn't on the ERT."

"You were in the gang squad though, weren't you?" asked Michael.

"Yes, but it's not called the gang squad either," said Coach T. "Before I became a liaison officer I was a member of what's called the Special Enforcement Unit," he explained. "Our job was to stop organized criminals. Some are gang members."

"That's awesome!" said Jun. "Being undercover, driving fast, arresting bad guys? I would love that job!"

"There were some interesting moments," Coach T said. "But it wasn't like what you see on TV. We spent a lot of time on paperwork and on our computers. Often we would sit in our cars and watch a house or a business for hours. And still not see anything."

"Yeah, but it had to be more exciting than being a liaison officer," said Michael. "Why would anybody want to work with kids when you could go after gangs? Isn't that kinda… boring?"

Coach T laughed. "Actually, I think being a liaison officer is one of the most important things we do in the RCMP. I work with high school and elementary kids, and I help them make good choices. It's a lot more rewarding keeping kids out of gangs than arresting them once they are in them."

"And you get to coach the best soccer team in the world!" said Junior.

"That is true as well," said Coach T. "The very best team!"

10
The First Game

"Warm up, Eagles," said Coach T when they arrived at Griffith Park Elementary. "The game starts in ten minutes."

"In a circle, guys," said Claude. "Do what I do." To everyone's approval, Coach T had named Claude the captain. Claude never got too excited, and was always encouraging. That he was one of the best players on the team didn't hurt.

Dylan tried to sort out his feelings about the game. Part of him wanted to play, to blow off steam. But another part of him wanted to quit, to run home and lock himself in his room.

As he stretched, Dylan looked at the Griffith Park team. They were called the Dragons and their uniforms were yellow. Their players were a mixture of kids from all over the world, just like at Grandview. The school looked like Grandview, too, and their field was identical — a slightly uneven, ugly dirt field.

"Let's have a good game," said Coach T as the

players huddled up. "Play hard, play safe, play fair. Jun and Abdul, you start on the sidelines and I'll sub you in later. We'll play 4, 4 and 2. Griffith Park won the coin toss so they start with the ball."

In their 4-4-2 formation, they had four defenders, four midfielders and two strikers. Abbas and Dylan were up front, Claude, Mo, Junior and Jake played midfield. William, Steven, Alvin and Carlos were defence. Michael was the goalie.

"Bring it in for a cheer, boys!" said Coach T.

"One! Two! Three! Go Eagles!"

The Grandview team took their positions on the field and waited for the whistle to start the game. Dylan was nervous. He was rusty. He had no idea how things would go.

The referee tweeted the whistle and the first thirty-minute half started. The Griffith Park forward passed the ball back to a midfielder. The rest of their team moved up the field, getting ready to attack. The midfielder made a nifty move and got past Junior. But Claude read the play, ran over to support, and quickly stripped the Griffith Park player of the ball. Now Grandview was on the offensive.

"Go!" Claude shouted. Abbas and Dylan raced toward the Griffith Park goal, Abbas on the right, Dylan on the left. Claude faked a move and booted the ball, a beautiful kick that rose in the air and landed half a metre away from Abbas. A Griffith

Park defender raced toward Abbas, but Abbas saw him coming. When the defender was just a few steps away, Abbas chipped the ball to Dylan.

It was a perfect pass. Dylan took the ball nervously. It was the first time in ages he was actually playing a real game. He took a deep breath and ran toward the Griffith Park net.

Maybe he wasn't that rusty after all, thought Dylan. It felt good to play.

Dylan looked down the field, toward the Griffith Park net. There was only one defender standing in his way. Dylan raced toward him, then quickly darted to the right, easily beating the defender. Five metres from the goal Dylan booted the ball at the upper right corner of the net. The goalie stood helpless as the ball rocketed past him. The game was barely three minutes old and it was 1–0 Grandview. It was the fastest goal Dylan had ever scored.

"Awesome!" cheered Claude as Dylan ran back to centre field.

"Thanks. Good pass, Abbas," Dylan added. The ref restarted the game. This time Griffith Park pushed forward, a striker running toward the Grandview goal. The Griffith Park player was fast, but Jake was faster. He stripped the ball and quickly passed it down the field. The ball bounced awkwardly over the uneven dirt field.

Dylan took the bouncing ball, ran a few metres, then passed it quickly across the field to Abbas. Not to be outdone by Dylan, Abbas sprinted toward the Griffith Park goalie and faked a shot to the left. When the goalie jumped, Abbas tapped the ball smartly to the right hand corner of the net. Ten minutes into the game it was Grandview: 2, Griffith Park: 0.

By halftime the score was Grandview: 4, Griffith Park: 1. Dylan had scored one of the other goals, a terrific shot that went through the goalie's legs. Jake scored as well, with Claude getting two assists.

Griffith Park's only goal in the half had come from a penalty shot after Carlos had accidently touched the ball with his hand. The Griffith Park player drilled the ball hard on the ground to the left. Michael guessed correctly and made a flying leap, but he missed the ball by a fingernail.

"Excellent job, boys!" Coach T said happily as the halftime break ended. "Let's have a great second half."

Jun and Abdul subbed in for Alvin and Junior. The boys took their positions, the ref blew the whistle and the second half began.

Just like in the first half, Grandview controlled the play. Within five minutes Dylan scored again, this time with a header from another great pass from Claude. It was only the second time in his life Dylan had scored a hat trick and he felt good — very good. Dylan hadn't played a competitive soccer game in months, but he still had it. More than that, the Grandview team was very good. Maybe as good as his old team at Regent Heights.

Golden Goal

When the final whistle blew, Grandview won their first game of the season 7–2. The boys hugged each other, shook hands with the Griffith Park players and huddled up on the sidelines.

"Good game, boys," said Coach T.

"Good? Don't you mean great, Coach?" laughed Mo. "With Abbas, Claude and Dylan who can beat us?"

"Regent Heights will certainly try," said Coach T. "They're district champions, remember? We'll see how good you really are next Monday."

⚽ ⚽ ⚽

"You played well," Abbas said to Dylan.

Abbas was happy. All the boys were happy. The team was in a great mood as they walked back to their school. Even the cold January rain couldn't dampen their spirits.

"You both did," said Coach T. "You two could very well be the best forwards in the school district. I'm glad you've been able to fix things. Ms. Bhullar told me what happened in the gym."

"Thanks, Coach T," Dylan said. But he was hardly paying attention. The fight seemed ages ago to Dylan. He didn't have bad feelings toward Abbas, not anymore. It was Emmanuel and Tony he was angry with.

See you when we play your school in a couple weeks, Emmanuel had said that day in the mall. Dylan's heart raced when he thought about it. He would have the best game of his life and beat Regent badly. That would show Emmanuel and Tony! He realized he wanted to get back at them and that was how he'd do it. Revenge. That was the word. His friends had lied to him, abandoned him. Dylan would get his revenge.

All week Dylan played harder than he'd ever done before. At practice, at lunch and recess and after school, Dylan lived with his soccer ball.

"It's terrible outside," said Ms. Jorgensen on Wednesday. "I can't remember when I've seen so much rain. You can stay inside today at lunch if you want."

It had been awful all week, wet and windy and cold, but that didn't stop Dylan or the other boys.

"This is Vancouver!" said Dylan. "It always rains here in winter."

"You really want to beat your old school don't you?" Claude asked Dylan as they put on their coats. They stepped out onto the field, which looked more like a swimming pool than a soccer field in places.

"Yeah, I guess so." Dylan hadn't said anything to his team about meeting his old friends in Supersports. He hadn't even told his mom. He didn't want to give her more to worry about.

"Don't worry. We'll play well," Claude promised Dylan. "We're teammates — and friends. If it's important to you, it's important to me."

"Thanks," Dylan said. To his surprise, he felt like crying at Claude's kind words.

After the mall, Dylan had begun to feel something else as well as anger. There must be something wrong with him, he'd thought. Why else would Tony and Emmanuel have excluded him? Dylan felt *worthless*, like he didn't deserve friends. Yet here was Claude, a boy he'd only known for a very short time, being nicer to him than people he'd known his entire life. Dylan was confused, and didn't quite know what to think.

11
Regent Heights Comes to Play

"How are you feeling about the game today?" Dylan's mom asked early Monday morning. "I wish I could come but I won't get home in time and I haven't been there long enough to ask for time off yet."

"It's no big deal, Mom, "Dylan said. "It's only our second game of the season. It's not like it's a playoff or anything."

"If you say so, Dylan." Her tone made Dylan think she didn't quite believe him. "Anyway, have some breakfast. You'll need your energy today."

Dylan had hardly eaten all week. "I'm not really that hungry," he said, picking at a piece of toast.

Dylan's nerves were alive and his whole body seemed to vibrate. All he could think about was the game.

"I don't care if you're hungry or not," his mom said firmly. "Besides, I made scrambled eggs and they're not going to waste."

Dylan ate a few hurried forkfuls before rushing to the front door, soccer ball in his hand.

The school day was the slowest one of his life. Social Studies and Math dragged by, and Dylan nearly cheered when the recess bell rang. The boys sprinted out to the field to play a quick game. They reluctantly came in when the bell rang. At lunch, Ms. Pucci served them hamburgers. The boys wolfed them down, eager to get outside.

"Play hard, play safe, play fair," said Claude, playing the role of Coach T. "We have a big game today. Let's get ready."

For the next forty-five minutes the boys peppered Michael with shots. They practised corner kicks, set plays and passes. They were *on*. Dylan felt it, they all did. When lunch ended, the boys left the field sweaty, tired and confident they were going to beat Regent.

Dylan settled into his desk and got out his science book. Two hours from now he would meet Tony and Emmanuel on Grandview's field. Two hours from now he would get his revenge.

The entire school was excited about the game. All the kids, from Kindergarten to Grade 7 were on the sidelines. As he waited for the Regent team to arrive, Dylan could hardly breathe, he was so nervous. When the first carload of Regent players showed up, he felt he would explode.

"Huddle up, boys," said Coach T as the rest of the Regent players arrived. "I know you're excited, but remember that this is only the second game of the season. We have a lot of soccer left to play."

"Let's get these guys!" said Jake. "We can beat them!"

The entire team cheered loudly in response.

"Yes, you can," said Coach T, "but Regent's the best in the district for a reason. This is going to be a tough test and you'll have to play as a team. With Alvin and William sick, we don't have subs today. We can't afford to make mistakes or have anyone get hurt. Play hard, play safe, play fair. And show them what the Eagles can do."

"One! Two! Three! Eagles!" cheered the boys as they took the field.

Dylan lined up against Tony. "Hey," Tony said. Dylan ignored him.

"What kind of field is this?" sneered a Regent player named Ethan. "I feel like I'm playing on a farm! You guys should be the ducks or chickens, not the Eagles."

The rest of the Regent players laughed at the comment. They had a beautiful turf field, proper benches and lights. Dylan was more aware than ever that the Grandview field was uneven and dirty, and still had puddles.

"Yeah, chickens," said Tony, chuckling as a Regent midfielder began to cluck.

"They're not chickens. They're losers," sneered a red-headed midfielder. His name was Liam. Dylan remembered not liking him very much. Liam was a bully with sharp features and beady eyes. He reminded Dylan of a rat. "Loser field, loser uniforms, loser school, loser kids."

"What did you say?" asked Dylan, his face red with anger. He looked over to Abbas. Dylan was sure that Abbas would be as angry at the comments as he was. Instead the other forward acted as if he hadn't heard a thing.

"Ref? Are you going to do something about this?" asked Coach T from the sidelines. The Regent coach and parents had either not heard the awful comments — or were ignoring them.

"That's enough, boys," said the referee. "Tell your team to be a little more respectful," the ref added to Coach Alvarez. "I'll red card the next player who says something out of turn."

"Regent: focus on the game," Alvarez said. But Dylan could tell by the smile on his old coach's face that he thought the comments were funny.

Dylan's cheeks burned. Never in his life had he wanted to beat a team so badly. *Blow the whistle, ref,* he thought. *Let's get started.*

Grandview won the toss. The whistle blew and Dylan back-heeled the ball to Claude. Just as they'd practiced, Dylan sprinted down the left side while Abbas kept pace on the right. Dylan looked downfield toward the Regent goal and Emmanuel, their goalie.

"Dylan!" shouted Claude. He booted the ball high in the air. As always, Claude's pass was flawless. It cleared the heads of the midfielders and bounced high in the dirt. Dylan picked it up and sped toward the goal. Two Regent defenders, Christian and Owen, were all that stood between Dylan and Emmanuel.

"Here!" cried Abbas. Dylan looked quickly to his right. Sure enough, Abbas was wide open. A quick flick of the ball was all it would take, and from that range there was no way Abbas would miss. But then Dylan wouldn't get to score on his former friend. Besides, Dylan was better than Christian and Owen, and he knew it.

There was a gap between the defenders. Dylan raced toward it, eager to clear the space and blast the ball into the net. The distance closed quickly, five metres, then three. Soon Dylan would be clear. One more step and he would shoot. *Try to save this, Emmanuel,* he thought. But out of nowhere Owen's foot reached out and took the ball away from him. Dylan stumbled, fell hard into the dirt, and rolled to a stop just a metre away from Emmanuel.

"You're gonna have to do better than that to score on me," Emmanuel grinned.

Dylan ignored him. He hurried back down the field, not looking at Abbas. If Dylan had passed they would be celebrating a goal. Instead, Dylan watched in horror as Owen launched the ball downfield to the rat-faced midfielder Liam. Liam passed it to Tony, who easily beat Carlos, then blasted the ball past Michael into the back of the net. It was 1–0 for Regent Heights.

"Come on, boys, you can do this," encouraged Coach T as play started again.

For the next fifteen minutes, the two teams played a scrappy, defensive game. Nobody seemed able to get past the other team's midfielders, and they shared possession equally. Suddenly, Jun won a contest for the ball with a Regent forward. He lobbed it up to Claude. Claude kicked it to Dylan who had anticipated the play and moved to an open space on the field.

The ball bounced high on the dirt. Dylan controlled it with his chest and rushed to the wing as Abbas and Claude followed. Christian and Owen dashed toward him, cutting off the angle, forcing Dylan toward the sidelines.

I'll show you, Emmanuel, he thought as the goal line approached. "Dylan!" cried Claude. "Over here!" Both Claude and Abbas were wide open. But all Dylan could think about was slamming the ball over Emmanuel's head himself.

I can do this, he thought. *I've scored from sharper angles before.* Fifteen metres away from the goal line, far to the left of the net, Dylan leaned into the ball. He kicked harder than he'd ever kicked before. The ball flew in the air like a rocket toward the net — then sailed harmlessly out of touch a good two metres wide.

"Dylan! We were open!" said Claude in disbelief.

"I thought I had the angle," Dylan said weakly, hurrying back to position.

With just seconds to go in the half, Regent Heights scored again. It was Liam who scored with a low, bouncing kick that rolled off Michael's fingertips and over the line. Regent Heights: 2, Grandview: 0.

"Halftime!" the ref shouted, blowing his whistle.

12
Red Card

Laughing and congratulating Liam, the Regent Heights team left the field, their mood much lighter than Grandview's. The Eagles were frustrated. They were playing as well as Regent Heights and at the very least the score should be tied.

Coach T pulled Dylan aside. "Listen, Dylan, I get it," he said. "They're your old team and your old friends and you want to beat them. But both times you chose a low percentage shot when you should have passed to a teammate who was open. This is a team game. We can't afford to be selfish, even if we think we have good reasons."

"It's not like that, Coach," Dylan protested. But he didn't even believe himself. "I thought I had the shot."

"You're a completely different player from last week," said Coach T. "Your head's not in the game. Honestly, Dylan, if Alvin and William were here, I'd bench you right now for your own good. But we can't afford to go down to ten players. You're going to play defence for the second half. Carlos will move up to midfield, and Claude will play forward."

"Defence?" Dylan was horrified. He'd been a striker for as long as he'd played soccer.

"Defence," Coach T repeated. "You're playing like a one-man-show. We can win this game. But they've gotten to you. You have to shake it off. If you can't, we don't have a chance of beating these guys."

⚽ ⚽ ⚽

When the second half started, it looked like Grandview would pull even. The Regent players had laughed at Grandview's dirt field, but they were having a hard time playing on it. The Regent players were used to smooth, even turf where balls didn't take strange bounces or slow down in a patch of mud. These things didn't bother the Grandview players one bit.

The Grandview players were working hard as well. Carlos wasn't as good a midfielder as Claude, but five minutes into the second half, he made a great tackle. He took the ball and kicked it through the legs of a Regent Heights player, right to Abbas's feet. Abbas took off. He faked a shot that pulled Emmanuel off his line, then slid the ball to Claude, who tapped it into the open net. The Grandview team and the students on the sidelines cheered. Regent Heights: 2, Grandview: 1.

Red Card

With twenty-five minutes left in the game, the momentum had shifted. The Grandview team seemed to have shaken off their nerves, and were playing with confidence. Regent Heights was the best team in the district, but Grandview was now only one goal down and they were playing like they could win.

"We got this, guys!" Claude said, encouraging the team as play started again. Every one of the Grandview Eagles was pumped. Everyone except Dylan. He had dreamed of this day, of getting back at Tony and Emmanuel. Instead he'd been moved from forward to defence. Instead he was playing terribly. Dylan was desperate. There had to be something he could do.

A few minutes later he had his chance. Liam sprang Tony free with a smart pass. Tony deftly avoided the Grandview midfielders and headed toward the net. Dylan clenched his teeth and squared up to face Tony.

Tony was good. But Dylan had played with him for years. Dylan knew all of his moves. Tony usually did a shoulder fake to the left to throw the defender off-balance. Then he'd drag the ball sharply to the right, and race wide-open to the net. It wasn't fancy, but Tony was fast, and most times he managed to fool the defender. But Dylan wasn't most defenders. He would stop Tony in his tracks.

Tony raced right toward Dylan, as if he wanted to show his old friend who was better. There was no way Dylan was going to let that happen. Dylan backed up into the penalty box, waiting for Tony to make his move. Suddenly Tony was there, so close Dylan could see right in his eyes. *I have you*, Dylan thought, his heart pounding in his chest.

Tony ducked his shoulder, just as Dylan thought he would. Dylan wasn't biting. Instead he lunged at Tony, swinging his foot where he knew the ball would be. But instead of booting the ball, he hit something else. Tony shouted out in pain and collapsed onto the field, grabbing his shin.

"Tweet!" went the ref's whistle as his other hand reached into his pocket. Dylan was confused. *Why is the ref showing me a red card? Why is he pointing to the penalty spot?*

Then Dylan realized what he'd done. He'd hurt Tony. His kick was a blatant, ugly foul. He was being sent off and Regent Heights were getting a penalty kick. A red card! He'd never had a red card in his entire life. In a daze, Dylan walked to the sidelines.

He left the field and stared back at Tony, who was only now getting up with the help of Coach Alvarez and another Regent Heights player. Coach T was saying something to Dylan, but all he heard though the blood rushing in his ears was a distant mumble.

Back on the field, Liam lined up at the penalty spot. Tony was the best penalty kicker on the Regent Heights team. But with Tony's leg hurt, Coach Alvarez had decided someone else should take the kick. Michael stood on the line, knees flexed, ready to dive.

"Tweet!" went the whistle again. The entire Grandview team and the students on the sidelines held their breath. Liam leaned into the ball and drilled it high to the left. Michael had guessed wrong. He jumped to the right, leaving the net wide open. There was no way Liam could miss. Regent Heights: 3, Grandview: 1.

Whatever confidence the Grandview Eagles had, it quickly disappeared. Down to ten players and losing by two again, they were easy victims for Regent, who easily scored three more goals.

The fulltime whistle blew. The final score was 6–1 for Regent Heights. It wasn't just a loss for Grandview. They had been absolutely destroyed.

"Go shake hands, guys," said Coach T. Win or lose, sportsmanship was important to him. Heads hanging low, the Grandview Eagles lined up on the field. "You too, Dylan," said Coach T.

The thought of shaking his old friends' hands, of looking into their eyes after this defeat made Dylan want to throw up. Reluctantly, Dylan joined the line.

"I told you they were a bunch of losers," said Liam.

"Dirty too," said Tony, limping past, a scowl on his face. He didn't even pretend to shake Dylan's hand.

I'm so sorry, Tony, it was an accident. I didn't mean to hurt you, Dylan tried to say to Tony, but nothing came out. Instead, he walked back to the sidelines in silence.

"Eagles, huddle up," said Coach T. *About to give some sort of pep talk no doubt*, thought Dylan.

Whatever it was, Dylan wanted no part of it. A giant sob erupted in his throat. He was nearly in tears. And there was no way he would let Tony or Emmanuel — or even Abbas and Claude — see that. Without waiting to hear what Coach T was saying, Dylan sprinted off the field toward the school.

13
True Friends

His whole body shaking with tears, Dylan rounded the corner and slumped against the school's brick wall. He'd lost his dad, his home, his school and his friends. Even then, Dylan had somehow fooled himself into thinking that he could get over it. What a fool he'd been. Things would never be right again. Lost in his misery, he didn't hear footsteps approaching until somebody stood right in front of him.

Through his tears Dylan saw Abbas and Claude. "What do you want?" he sniffed. "To yell at me because I lost us the game? To call me a loser?"

Abbas said nothing. Instead, he slid down the wall and sat in silence beside Dylan. Claude sat down on Dylan's other side.

"I was born in Syria," Abbas finally said. "I was six when my family left because of the war. There were five of us. My mother and father, and my older brothers Naser and Ali. We crossed the border and lived in Turkey."

Dylan stopped crying and looked at Abbas. "In a refugee camp like Claude?"

"No. We lived in an apartment in a small town near the border. We didn't like it very much. My dad couldn't work. We couldn't go home to Syria, and it was against the law for us to leave Turkey. We were stuck. But at least I had my brothers. They were a lot older than me, but we were very close. We used to play soccer together all the time. They wouldn't let me win just because I was younger, either. I had to work very hard to score on them, especially Ali. Ali was a very good goalie."

"How did you get here?" asked Dylan.

"We lived in Turkey for almost five years," Abbas said. "We were getting desperate to find a better life. So my father decided that he would try to go to Europe. I hadn't even heard of Canada back then."

"If it was against the law how did he manage to leave?" Dylan asked, forgetting about his own sadness.

"If you had enough money you could get a ride on a boat to Greece," Abbas said. "So my father, Ali and Naser decided to go. They planned to settle in Norway or Germany or someplace. Any place better than where we were. Then they would get jobs, save up money and send for us. The trip to Greece was dangerous and very expensive, but my father said it was worth the risk. Besides, he told us they would be fine. My mother and I kissed my father and brothers goodbye. We were all crying, but my father said he would see us again soon.

And then they left. I went to play with some friends. A few hours later I went home. We were having dinner when a man came to the door."

"What did he want?" Dylan asked. An awful feeling was growing in his stomach.

Tears welled in Abbas's eyes. "He told us that the boat had sunk a few kilometres from shore. My father and my brothers had drowned. I couldn't believe what I was hearing. My mother fell to her knees and just screamed and cried."

Dylan listened in silence. He knew about bad days like that all too well.

"It was the worst day of my life."

Abbas continued after a while. "A few months later, my mother and I were asked by United Nations people if we wanted to come to Canada. That's how I came here."

"Why are you telling me this now?" Dylan asked. "You haven't said a word about your family to anyone before."

Abbas turned to Dylan. "I heard that boy from the other team when he called you a loser. I am still learning English, but I know that the same word can mean different things. His meaning was to insult you. To say that you were no good. Yes, you are a loser. But not how those other boys meant it. I am also a loser. So is Claude, Mo and everyone on our team. We are losers because we have lost things and people that are important to us. We are losers because we have lost our homes, family, even our countries. But we have survived. We have overcome that loss. And because of that we are stronger than they can ever be. It isn't a bad thing to be a loser. It is something to be proud of."

Dylan's tears returned. "But how do we overcome it? How did you get past losing your parents and your brothers?" Dylan had lost his father, but not his whole family, not his whole country. He couldn't believe he could ever have the sort of strength Abbas was talking about, the kind Abbas and Claude showed every day.

"I was angry about it, just like you," replied Abbas. "I still am sometimes. I used to fight all the time. But my friends understand me and help. That's what friends do."

"I had friends at Regent Heights. But they left me," said Dylan.

"Then they were never really your friends. True friends don't leave when things get tough," Abbas said. "Friends support you. And we are your friends."

Dylan ran an arm across his eyes to dry his tears.

"See you tomorrow at school?" Claude asked, standing up. "And at practice too, right? Six more games before the playoffs. I have a feeling we will get another chance to play Regent Heights before the season is over."

"Yes," Dylan replied, a faint smile on his face. "I'll see you tomorrow."

⚽ ⚽ ⚽

True Friends

Dylan told his mom everything when she got home. He told her about meeting Emmanuel and Tony at the mall, and how he'd not been invited to the party. He told her about the game, and what Abbas said afterwards. When he was done, it felt like a huge weight was taken off his chest.

"I just feel so bad you didn't tell me about Tony and Emmanuel," his mom said. She brushed tears away from the corner of her eyes. "If you want to stay in touch with those guys I'm sure we can find a way. I could find an inexpensive phone for you. I can't afford anything fancy or even a SIM card right now. But there's wireless and I'm sure…"

"It's okay, Mom," Dylan said. "Everyone I want to talk to these days is either in this apartment or at school."

"I'm so proud of you, son," his mom said, hugging him tightly. "Abbas and Claude sound like very nice friends to have. The kind who will stick with you, especially when things are tough."

His mom was right, he realized. When he was at his lowest it was Abbas and Claude who had come to see if he was all right. It was Abbas and Claude who understood, who really understood, what he was going through. And it was Abbas and Claude who accepted him for who he was and forgave him for screwing up in the game. They were friends, the very best kind.

True friends.

14
The Dinner Party

When Dylan woke up the next morning he found himself looking forward to school. He ate a quick breakfast, kissed his mom goodbye and raced down the stairs to Salisbury. He arrived at school thirty minutes before class started. But he wasn't the first one there. Abbas, Claude and half a dozen other boys were already on the field.

At first, Dylan was worried about how the other boys on the team would treat him. Everyone knew they lost the game against Regent because of him. But none of the boys gave Dylan a hard time about it. He thought about how his old teammates would have reacted if he was the cause of losing a game. The understanding the Grandview team showed certainly wouldn't have happened back at his old school.

"Don't worry about yesterday, Dylan," said Michael, slapping him on the back. "Everyone has a bad game sometimes. You should see some of the goals I've let in."

The Dinner Party

"All of us could have played better yesterday," added Claude.

"We have some work to do for sure," said Mo. "Claude's feeling is right. We'll be meeting Regent Heights again in the playoffs and then we'll show them just what the Grandview Eagles can do!"

At lunchtime Dylan rushed down to the cafeteria, ready to eat before going outside to play soccer. He gobbled down his fun bun (Ms. Bhullar was right — it was just a cheese sandwich and not much fun at all). Then he raced out onto the field to play with the rest of the team.

Dylan had never played so much soccer in his life. The team practised Tuesday and Thursday with Coach T. The boys played pickup games every lunch and recess, and after-school scrimmages on Monday, Wednesday and Friday. It was a great week, but the best part of it had nothing to do with soccer.

"My mom has invited you guys over to our place on Friday for dinner," Abbas told Dylan and Claude on Wednesday morning. "And your mom, Dylan. And Claude's sister, too. Six o'clock?"

"Great, thanks!" said Dylan. He couldn't remember the last time he'd gone to a friend's house. He was excited, and he knew his mom would be too.

"We will come for sure," said Claude.

"Good!" Abbas grinned. "My mom will be happy to feed everyone!"

Golden Goal

⚽ ⚽ ⚽

On their way to Abbas's place, Dylan and his mom stopped at the green grocer on Grandview to pick up a bouquet of flowers. "You should always bring a little gift for the hostess," his mom said. "It's bad manners not to."

Abbas and his mother lived in a basement suite on Linden Avenue, halfway between the school and Dylan's place. The Wests arrived at the same time that Claude and his sister appeared at the door.

"My name is Julie," said Claude's sister, introducing herself.

"Erin, Erin West," said Dylan's mom. "This is Dylan."

"A pleasure to meet you, Dylan," said Julie, "though I feel as if I already know you. Claude talks about you all the time."

"I know what you mean." Dylan's mom smiled. "All I ever hear from my son is Claude this and Abbas that!"

The door opened. "Please, come in." Dylan hadn't seen Amira Wassef, Abbas's mom, since the day of the fight. She was younger than his own mom, Dylan realized. Today she wore a light-blue *hijab*.

The basement suite was even smaller than the Wests' apartment. But it felt warm and comfortable. And it was full of wonderful smells that made Dylan's mouth water.

The Dinner Party

"I hope you guys are hungry," said Abbas. "My mom likes to cook and she wants you to try some traditional Syrian foods."

Dylan had never eaten such food back in his old neighbourhood. The meal was one of the best he'd ever had. "This is called *yabraq*: vine leaves stuffed with rice and meat," Mrs. Wassef said, passing around the first dish. The yabraq was followed by falafel chickpea balls and kebabs of skewered chunks of meat.

"This is absolutely delicious!" said Dylan's mom, and everyone around the table agreed. "And how is soccer going, by the way?" she asked Claude. "You had a tough loss on Monday."

"Yes, but we won't lose again," Claude said confidently. "I have a feeling."

"And if we win all of our games we will make the playoffs. And we will play Regent Heights in the final," Abbas said. "They got lucky this week. It won't happen again."

"If you do, I'll get off work early and watch," Dylan's mom said.

"I will be there as well," Julie promised.

"I will come too," Mrs. Wassef added. "But first you must eat dessert." With that, she went into the tiny kitchen and brought back a plate of sweet pastries. "*Baqlawah*," she said. "Very good."

"I know these as baklava," Dylan's mom said. "And I love them!"

"I don't care what they are called," said Claude, helping himself to a second large piece. He had nearly inhaled his first helping. "They are delicious in any language!"

"Claude and I will have you all over to our place for dinner, soon," said Julie, handing Claude a napkin. The boys were licking the sweet honey syrup from the baqlawah off their fingers. "I will make Congolese food for you!"

"And then it's our turn," said Dylan's mom. "But I'm afraid I won't be able to make anything as terrific as this!"

"Are you kidding, Mom?" said Dylan. "Your spaghetti and meatballs are the best in the world!"

"Spaghetti and meatballs sounds very good," said Mrs. Wassef. "We would love to come."

An hour later, the dishes were done and the adults were finishing cups of tea. It was time to go home.

"Thank you so much, Amira," said Dylan's mom, hugging her. "It was the nicest evening I've had in ages. And the meal was terrific!"

"You should come and work in the school, Mrs. Wassef," Claude said.

"Thank you, Claude. But I was a chemist in Syria, not a teacher."

"Who said anything about teaching?" Claude grinned. "You should run the cafeteria. No offence to Ms. Pucci, but I'd take kebabs and *baqlawah*, over fun buns any day!"

15
One Point for the Playoffs

The following Monday was Grandview's last away game. The team walked the half hour to Salish Elementary in a cold, driving rain.

"Nothing fancy, boys," said Coach T before they took the field. "Forget about the game with Regent Heights. Play hard, support each other and have fun."

The terrible weather didn't affect their play. A few minutes into the game Abbas stripped a Salish player of the ball and drove toward the net alone. With his usual perfect aim, Abbas fired the ball high and to the left of the goalie, putting Grandview up 1–0.

"Great shot," said Claude when they took their positions to restart the game. Within minutes Abbas took a pass from Jake and made a hard shot. It skipped over the muddy surface of Salish's dirt field, but just missed the net. Abbas was having the game of the season and Dylan was glad. Dylan was trying to put the game against his old school behind him. But his confidence was low and he spent most of the first half getting rid of the ball as soon as he touched it. The last thing Dylan wanted was for the team to lose another game because of him.

Grandview led 1–0 at the half.

"Dylan," said Coach T, pulling him aside. "You're playing like you're scared of the ball."

"I just don't want to be the reason we lose again, Coach T," he said earnestly.

"Let go of the Regent Heights game," Coach T replied. "If we're going to win, we need everyone to play their best. Abbas is having a great game but he can't win this thing himself. He needs you out there — we need you."

Dylan's first touch of the second half came a minute after kickoff. He was tempted to get rid of the ball right away. But Coach T's words were still in his mind. He took a second to compose himself and dribbled down the field. He crossed it over to Abbas, who made a great shot. The ball sailed past the goalie into the net. Grandview: 2, Salish Elementary: 0.

"That's better!" cheered Coach T.

"Nice pass," Abbas said.

"Thanks." Dylan felt a weight lift from his chest. He'd played the ball. And he hadn't made a mistake that cost the team the game. Instead he'd earned an assist.

The game ended 4–0 for Grandview. Abbas scored a hat trick and Mo got the other, a beautiful header on a cross from Claude. Dylan had a great game himself, assisting on two of the goals. The weather was worse than ever as they walked back to school, but their spirits were high. For everyone, including Dylan, the Regent Heights disaster was behind them.

"Three games down, five to go," said Claude. "I have a feeling this is going to be our best season ever."

Claude was right. Grandview won a rematch against Griffith Park 3–0. That was followed by a win against Fifth Avenue, and ties against Confederation and University Hill. The Grandview Eagles were having the best season in the school's history. But none of it mattered if they lost their last game of the season against Brentford.

"Huddle up, boys," said Coach T. They were wrapping up their last practice of the regular season. It was a beautiful Thursday in early March and the worst of winter was behind them. The cherry trees that lined the edge of the field were blooming, and daffodils and crocuses were growing in the flowerbeds. It hadn't rained for more than a week and their field was dry for the first time in months. It was as uneven and lumpy as ever, but the boys knew and loved every inch of it.

"We play Brentford on Monday," Coach T reminded the team, not that anyone needed reminding. The game was all they had been talking about for a week. "We have four wins, two draws and a loss," he said. "A great job so far, but we have to win or at least draw against Brentford to make the playoffs. Only the top four teams in each zone move on, and right now we are tied with Salish for fourth. Just one point and we make the playoffs."

"No problem, Coach!" piped up Mo. "We can beat Brentford easy!"

"I don't know," said Alvin nervously. "My cousin goes there. They haven't lost a game all season and are pretty good."

"They are good," agreed Coach T. "But if you play as a team you have a very good chance. Work together and believe in yourselves. Who knows how far we can go?"

The boys made the most of their two days off. They met at the school on both Saturday and Sunday to practise. They played soccer until the sun went down and they could hardly see the ball.

After what seemed the longest weekend of Dylan's life, Monday finally arrived.

"I never thought I'd ever say it, but I'm glad the weekend's over," said Steven.

"Me too," Dylan agreed. The day dragged by and Dylan's nerves grew. When the bell finally rang, the players sprinted down to the field. Once again, it seemed like every student at Grandview Community School had come out to watch. When the whistle sounded to start the game, Dylan felt as if he would explode.

Ten minutes into play Dylan knew they were in for a fight. Brentford wasn't as talented as Regent Heights, or even their own team. But their players were big, tough and fast. Dylan was finding that out the hard way.

"Here!" Dylan cried, streaking up the middle. Jun fed him an excellent pass and he started to run downfield. Dylan thought he was all alone until he saw a flash from the corner of his eye. The next thing he knew he was on the ground, stripped cleanly of the ball by one of the biggest kids he had ever seen.

The game went back and forth with nobody scoring. Brentford's strikers broke through Claude, Junior, Mo and Jake once or twice, but were stopped by Steven and Jun.

The first half ended with Grandview: 0, Brentford: 0.

"I feel like I've gone twelve rounds with Manny Pacquiao!" said Jake, limping off the field, both his legs bruised.

"I feel like I've spent half an hour in a tornado," Mo added.

All of the Grandview players were bumped and bruised. Most had scrapes on their legs from falling onto the dirt field. It was the toughest game they'd played.

"Well done," beamed Coach T as the team picked up their water bottles. "No matter what the final score is, I couldn't be prouder."

Dylan was still sweating when the ref blew the whistle to start the second half. "Thirty minutes to go," he told Abbas. "We can do this."

16
The Save

The second half of the game against Brentford was even more physical. Most of the play happened in the middle of the field, with neither side able to break through.

"There can't be more than ten minutes left," panted Claude. "At first I wanted to win, but I'll be more than happy with a draw. These guys are good!"

It was clear why neither team wanted to lose. A win or a tie would give Brentford first place in the South Zone. A place in the playoffs was on the line for Grandview. Pride was on the line for one team — survival for the other.

With a minute to go it seemed certain the game would end in a scoreless draw and both teams would be happy. But then a Brentford defender stole the ball from Abbas with a nifty slide tackle. The defender quickly booted the ball up to midfield, and deked past Claude. Normally Claude could have stopped him, but he had been sprinting up and down the field for almost an hour. Claude was exhausted and stumbled in a soft spot on the field. Usually it was visiting players who had problems with Grandview's bumpy field. This time it was Claude.

The Brentford midfielder sprinted forward and lobbed the ball high into the air. The Grandview crease was full of players from both teams, bumping, pushing each other to get in position as the ball dropped to the ground. In the net, Michael bounced up and down on his heels, ready to dive into action.

The ball was going to land between Jun and the Brentford striker. Jun bent down, looking to gain control of the ball with his chest. Then the unspeakable happened. The ball took an awkward bounce on the dirt and spun to the left. Instead of hitting Jun square in the chest, it smacked him in the elbow.

"Tweet!" blew the whistle as the Brentford players cheered. Grandview players and fans alike groaned in dismay as Jun dropped to his knees in disbelief. He hadn't meant to touch the ball with his arm. But since it happened, and in the box, it was an automatic penalty shot for Brentford. And there was almost no time left on the clock.

It was only the second penalty kick Grandview had surrendered all season. If Brentford scored, Grandview would not go to the playoffs. The Eagles' unbelievable season would end in heartbreak.

It was one of the most anxious moments of Dylan's life. This would be the last play of the game.

"You can do it, Michael!" Coach T called from the sidelines.

A Brentford player stood over the ball when the ref placed it on the penalty spot.

"You got this, Michael," Dylan said.

Their goalie squared up on the line, his knees flexed, his hands up, ready to pounce.

The ref blew the whistle. Every player on the field watched silently as the Brentford player ran up to the ball and launched it toward the net.

It was a good kick, hard and high to the right. Michael guessed correctly and leaped into the air in the same direction. The ball was going too fast to catch. But somehow Michael managed to punch the ball harmlessly over the bar.

The Grandview players erupted in cheers as the entire Brentford team stared at Michael in disbelief. It was one of the most spectacular saves any of them had ever seen.

"That was awesome!" said Dylan as he congratulated Michael.

The ref blew the fulltime whistle. When the shouting and cheering and hugging were done, the teams lined up and shook hands.

Back at the sidelines Coach T made the announcement the boys were waiting for.

"Welcome to the playoffs, boys! I've never been so happy to earn a tie! What made me the most proud was how you played. You worked together as a team and encouraged each other. You displayed great sportsmanship."

"When do the playoffs start?" asked Carlos.

"Our first game is a week from today. Since the district is divided into north and south zones, we will play each of the other three teams from the south that made the playoffs. The team with the best record plays the winner of the North Zone, a week from next Friday."

"Who do we play first?" asked Junior.

"Southlands," Coach T said. "And we get to play them at home."

"Uh oh," said Mo. "Southlands is good."

They hadn't played Southlands that season. But in the past, Grandview had never beaten them. Southlands had won the championship more times than any other school in the south.

"Yes, they are," replied Coach T. "But you guys are as good as any team in the district. If you keep playing like you have been, there's no reason you can't make the championship."

"Where is the championship game held?" Abbas asked.

Dylan knew the answer to that question. "The winner of the North Zone gets to host the final game this year," he explained. "Fifth Avenue was a South Zone finalist last year when I played for Regent. We beat them on their field."

"That's right," said Coach T. "It's the North Zone's turn to host. Dylan's old school hasn't lost a game all year and is looking very strong going into the playoffs. I'm pretty sure the winner of the South Zone will be playing for the district championship against Regent Heights — on their home field."

17
The Playoffs Begin

Mo was right. The Southlands Elementary soccer team was very good. Southlands even scored the first goal, a beautiful header in the middle of the first half of their game against Grandview. Grandview went into the halftime break losing 1–0, and the boys were panicked.

"Relax," Coach T said. "Just get out there and play your game. There's thirty minutes left to go. You can do this."

Abbas proved Coach T right ten minutes later.

"Abbas!" shouted Claude, drilling the ball up the right wing. Abbas took the ball and beat the Southlands defender. He sprinted to the net and blasted the ball along the ground to the goalie's left. Grandview: 1, Southlands: 1.

Grandview's nerves seemed to settle down after Abbas's goal, and all of them played with more confidence.

Fifteen minutes into the second half, Michael made a great save and booted the ball to Claude. The midfielder defending Claude slipped and Claude was left uncovered.

"Go!" shouted Dylan as Claude raced down the centre of the field. Dylan watched as Claude easily dribbled around a defender and fired into the net from point blank range. It was a beautiful shot, high and to the right of the helpless goalie. Grandview: 2, Southlands: 1.

Grandview didn't score again. But neither did Southlands. So when the fulltime whistle blew, the Eagles left the field as winners. Two more wins and they were in the finals.

"Good jobs, boys," said Coach T, high-fiving his players.

"Who do we play tomorrow?" asked Jun.

"Porter Street at home," he said. They lost to Brentford 2–1."

"What about Regent Heights? Did they win?" Dylan asked. The whole team waited for Coach T to text his friend. It wasn't just Dylan who had an interest in the outcome of that game.

Coach T nodded. "They won 5–0 over Burnaby Lake Elementary. But don't worry about what other teams are doing. Your only concern right now should be the game against Porter tomorrow."

The Porter Street Pirates put up a great fight. But they were no match for a Grandview Eagles team that played their best game of the season. Grandview won 6–2, with Abbas, Dylan, Jun and Abdul each scoring. The boys were tired but happy when they walked off the field.

The Playoffs Begin

One more win and they would make the district championships. But that win would not be easy. The game the next day would be a home rematch against Brentford, who had won their own game against Southlands with an impressive score of 4–0.

"Regent won as well, in case you were wondering," said Coach T before the boys could ask. "They are in the North Zone final tomorrow."

"I have a feeling that they'll win," Claude murmured to Dylan. "I told you we'd have another chance to play against them."

"First we have to beat Brentford," Dylan replied. "They're good, remember? We got a little lucky last time. If it wasn't for Michael making that crazy save we'd have lost for sure."

"But he did, and we didn't," said Claude. "And there is no way we will lose tomorrow either. I just know it."

No goals were scored in the first half of the game against Brentford. It was another tough, defensive game, with most of the play happening in the middle of the field. Abbas and Dylan kept trying to get free of the Brentford defence. But Brentford seemed to know exactly what they were trying to do. Their defenders matched Abbas and Dylan step for step.

"One goal is going to win this one, boys," said Coach T as the ref blew the whistle to start the second half.

"How are we going to score?" Dylan asked. "They're covering us really well. Abbas and I can't get free."

"Then somebody else is going to have to step up and score that goal, aren't they?

"Huddle up!" Coach T called. "Mo, Junior and Claude, pay extra careful attention."

The team huddled around their coach as he leaned down. When he had finished talking, Claude grinned and nodded.

The breakthrough came halfway into the second half. The Brentford defenders and midfielders kept focusing their efforts on defending against Dylan, Abbas and Claude. Those Grandview players were the scoring threat, and everyone knew it — which was just what Coach T was hoping for.

Michael made a save and kicked the ball to Claude. Claude raced as fast as he could downfield, just as he had a dozen times already in the game. Abbas and Dylan were both rushing down the right side of the field. Anticipating a pass to one of them, the Brentford defenders swarmed toward the three Grandview players. This time, however, Claude made a quick pass to Junior.

Junior was one of the fastest players on the team. He streaked down the undefended left side of the field with Carlos and Mo following in support. The Brentford players saw what was happening and tried to adjust. But before they could, Junior dropped the ball to Mo. Ten metres away from the goal, Mo thumped the ball at the net. It was a low, powerful shot that flew along the ground, skipping crazily along the lumpy field.

The Brentford goalie leapt toward the ball, stretching out his fingers. It was almost a brilliant save. But he missed it by a few centimetres. The ball rolled over the line and bounced to the back of the net. Grandview: 1, Brentford: 0.

Almost every Grandview student was watching the game, and their cheer was the loudest Dylan had ever heard. The boys mobbed Mo, as if he had scored the winning goal in the Olympics.

But the game wasn't over yet. When play started up again, Brentford pushed hard, desperate for an equalizer.

"Blow the whistle! Blow the whistle!" chanted the boys as the half wound down. Surely the game was over! But if the ref heard them he wasn't paying attention, and his watch was the only one that counted.

Dylan nearly fainted when a Brentford forward got off one last, desperate shot. It was from at least thirty metres out, but went high and straight, before dropping in the crease. Michael had guessed where the ball would go and positioned himself perfectly. He caught the ball on the bounce. The Grandview crowd erupted in cheers again while the players all held their breath, waiting for the whistle.

Michael kicked the ball. It went deep down the field right to Claude. The midfielder started toward the Brentford goal. But then they finally heard the long blast of the ref's whistle. Game over. Final score: Grandview: 1, Brentford: 0.

The home crowd went wild, hooting and hollering and running out onto the field to hug the players. Grandview was going to the district championships!

But against who? When the celebrations ended and the handshakes were over, the team gathered around Coach T.

"A friend of mine is watching the North Zone final," he said as he made a call. "Let's see who we are going to play." The call was quick. "Thanks. Call me back when you know." said Coach T before he hung up.

"What's up?" asked Jun. "Who are we going to play?"

"Regent Heights and Seacrest are tied 2–2. They're going into extra time," said Coach T. "They'll play ten minutes and unless there's a Golden Goal, they will go to penalty shots. My friend will text me the score when the game ends."

"Golden Goal?" Abbas looked confused.

"It's an old soccer phrase," explained Coach T. "It means the extra time is sudden-death. The Golden Goal is the one scored in extra time that wins the game."

"Golden Goal," Abbas repeated. He smiled. "I like that very much."

The next fifteen minutes seemed like the longest of Dylan's life. Part of him wanted Regent to win, but mostly he was rooting for his new school. Tony, Emmanuel and the rest of Regent Heights had embarrassed Dylan and Grandview Community School at the start of the season. Dylan wanted his team to have the chance to prove his old friends wrong.

Finally Coach T's phone chirped. "Game's over in the North Zone," he said. "No Golden Goal. It went to penalty shots."

"Who won?" shouted the boys impatiently. All were desperate to find out who they would play on Friday.

"The Regent Heights Knights," Coach T replied. "It seems Claude was right. You're going to have another chance to show them what the Grandview Eagles are made of after all."

18
The Trip to Regent Heights

The Grandview team drove in several cars heading north toward Regent Heights. Coach T took some of the players, as did Ms. Jorgensen, Ms. Pucci and Mr. Briscoe. Some parents came along as well. Dylan's mom left work early. There was no way she was missing the game. Mrs. Wassef and Claude's sister Julie felt the same way. They rode to Regent with Ms. Bhullar, as nervous as their children.

By car, Regent Heights was only twenty minutes away from Grandview. But it might as well have been in another world. There were no apartment buildings, no halal grocery stores in Regent Heights. All they could see were huge houses with large backyards that looked over the inlet and the North Shore Mountains.

"You lived here?" said Claude in disbelief. "Each one of these houses is bigger than my whole apartment building!"

"I never noticed," said Dylan truthfully. He'd lived

most of his life in this neighbourhood and had always taken things for granted.

As they travelled north on Shoreview Drive a very familiar street sign appeared ahead. Pinewood Crescent. His old street. If Coach T turned left and drove for just thirty seconds, they would see his old house. It was too much for Dylan. He shut his eyes and waited until he was sure they had passed the street by.

"You okay, Dylan?" Coach T asked.

"Just a little nervous about the game," he said. "I'll be fine."

As impressive as the houses were in Regent Heights, it was the school and soccer field that really blew the Grandview team away.

"Your old school is like a palace!" said Mo. "It looks more like a mall than a school!"

"And the field! It's turf! Proper benches and lights! Do the Whitecaps play here, too?" asked Abdul, only half-joking. "What about Barcelona?"

"No," said Dylan. "Just them."

As they pulled into the parking lot, the boys saw the Regent Heights players in their blue and silver uniforms warming up on the field. They weren't alone. Just as most of Grandview Community School's students had come out to watch the Eagles play at home, it looked like every student at Regent Heights was standing on the sidelines. They excitedly waited for the game to begin.

"Let's go, boys," said Coach T when the rest of the cars pulled in. Fifteen minutes before game time. "Get warmed up."

"These guys look pro," said Carlos.

Dylan could hear the worry in his teammate's voice. It was hard to argue with him. The Regent team's uniforms were new and sharp-looking. All the players and even the coach had matching track pants, jackets and shoes.

"It takes more than fancy clothes to be champions, Carlos," said Coach T. "You need dedication, talent and hard work. And you guys have more of those than any team I've ever seen."

"You heard Coach T," barked Claude. "We got this!" If he was intimidated by Regent Heights, he wasn't showing it.

"Hey, Dylan," sneered red-headed Regent player Liam, as Grandview took the field. "You and your loser friends are a long way from the farm, aren't you? This is what a real soccer field looks like, remember?"

"Ignore him, Dylan," said Michael. "He's not worth it."

"Ignore me all you want, losers," Liam said. "But you're gonna soon find out what real players can do on a real field instead of the farmyard you play on." Tony and Emmanuel stood beside Liam laughing. Neither one said hello to Dylan. They didn't give him the tiniest sign that they had ever been friends.

Like a wave crashing against the shore, all of Dylan's old feelings came back to him. His cheeks flushed red and he clenched his fists as Claude led them in stretches and warm-up drills. Never in his life had he wanted to win a game so much.

Dylan was nearly overcome by memories. He'd played on this field a million times since he was little. He had played here with his team and his dad. Now, his dad was gone and his old friendships were over. A place that had once been as familiar as his bedroom now seemed very strange to him.

"Dylan?" said Claude. "You don't look so good."

"I'm fine," Dylan replied. "It's just a little weird being back here, that's all."

"Two minutes, coaches," said the ref, checking his watch.

"Okay, Grandview, huddle up," Coach T said. The boys gathered around him, buzzing with nerves and energy. "I don't care if you win this game or not," he said. "As far as I'm concerned you have nothing to prove to me, to them, to anyone. You have done more than any coach could have hoped for this season, and I'm proud of each and every one of you."

"Nice speech, Coach T, but I wanna beat these guys bad!" said Junior. The whole team laughed and the tension slipped away.

"Then get out there and do it!" Coach T grinned. "Not for anyone but yourselves. Hands in," he said as he began his familiar cheer. "Play hard, play safe, play fair. Eagles on three."

"One! Two! Three! Eagles!" shouted the boys before they ran out onto the field.

"Visiting team, call it," said the ref as he flipped the coin into the air.

"Heads," said Claude, lining up against Tony, Regent's captain.

"Heads it is," said the ref, looking at the loonie lying in the turf. "Grandview kicks off."

"Enjoy it," said Tony to Claude. "The coin toss is the only thing you're going to win today."

19
The First Half

Five minutes into the game the Grandview Eagles were still nervous, but the Regent Heights Knights looked worried, too. It was clear from their trash talk that the Regent players had been expecting a quick goal and an easy game. Instead, they faced a hard-working Grandview team determined to win.

"Great work, defence!" encouraged Claude. William, Alvin and Carlos were like a solid wall, stopping the few Regent forwards who made their way through midfield. That included Tony, who couldn't hide his frustration when he was stripped of the ball by a nifty tackle from Carlos.

It was Grandview who almost scored first. Junior won a loose ball and lobbed it to Claude who sprinted downfield. Abbas and Dylan were closely marked and couldn't get free for a pass. So Claude took the shot himself. At the edge of the box he fired it toward Emmanuel. It would have landed in the back of the net except for the desperate lunge of a Regent Heights defender, who stuck out his foot and deflected it wide of the goal.

"Nice try, Claude," said Junior, running to take the corner kick.

The play went back and forth for the rest of the first half. There were several more chances for both teams. But when the boys returned to the sidelines for halftime, the score was tied 0–0.

"Go, Eagles!" cheered Dylan's mom from the sidelines, right where his dad used to watch. Dylan could almost see his dad standing beside her.

"Awesome half!" said Coach T, passing around the water bottles. "That was the best I've ever seen you play!"

"But we haven't scored yet," said Jake.

"Neither has Regent," Coach T reminded him. "And they were expecting a blow-out. You have nothing to lose. Just play your game and the chances will come."

One of those chances came less than five minutes into the second half. Jun passed the ball to Abbas who headed for the Regent goal. Dylan ran to the middle of the field. Moving steadily forward, Abbas fought off two Regent defenders. Dylan positioned himself at the top of the penalty box.

"Dylan!" shouted Abbas as he deked past a full-back. Abbas lobbed the ball right to where Dylan was standing. The pass was high and arcing. Dylan wasn't the best Grandview player when it came to headers, but this was a big, juicy chance to score with one.

Closer and closer the ball came. But just before Dylan was about to leap into the air, a sharp, stabbing pain erupted in his leg. He fell to the ground in agony, his leg aching, the wind knocked out of his lungs.

"No way! That's not a foul!" shouted Liam. "He fell down! I didn't touch him!"

But the referee blew the whistle, raised a yellow card and pointed to the penalty spot. Coach Alvarez was shouting at the ref, as were a dozen or so Regent Heights parents. They all seemed to agree that Liam had done nothing wrong. They were howling and screeching on the sidelines, calling the ref all sorts of names.

"They aren't very sportsmanlike," said Junior, watching the Regent Heights parents scream and shout.

"You don't know the half of it," said Dylan. The behaviour wasn't anything new to him. He knew that many of the parents acted like this at games. Pretty much the only Regent Heights parent who never did was his dad. Dylan had never much liked that behaviour when he played for Regent Heights. But he'd never seen how ugly it really was until he'd changed schools.

The referee wasn't buying it. He had seen Liam rake his shoe on the back of Dylan's leg hard enough to cause a large, rapidly bruising mark. "You do that again, number 16 and I'll send you off," the ref said.

"And you'd better control yourself and your parents, coach," he warned Coach Alvarez. "Or I'll give your team a red card right now and you'll finish the game down one player."

Coach T had rushed over to where Dylan had fallen. "Are you okay? Or should Abbas or Claude take the shot?" he asked. He checked Dylan's leg and helped him to his feet.

"I got this," Dylan said, clenching his teeth. He had just won a penalty shot! No way anybody was taking this kick but him. This was the chance Dylan had been waiting for.

Then he remembered what happened in the last game against Regent Heights.

"Maybe Abbas should take it, after all," Dylan said.

"Good call, Dylan," Coach T said. "You heard him, Abbas. You want to shoot?"

The smile on Abbas's face answered the question. Dylan watched as the referee placed the ball on the penalty spot. All the players but Grandview striker Abbas and Regent goalie Emmanuel cleared the box.

Dylan held his breath as Abbas lined up behind the ball. Abbas was a great shot. *He's taken a million penalty kicks in practice and never missed*, thought Dylan.

This was it. Dylan struggled to control his breath as the whistle blew. Emmanuel bobbed back and forth on the line. The crowd yelled, trying to distract Abbas. Dylan could hardly watch.

As if in slow motion, Abbas stepped toward the ball. He planted his right foot, swung back with his left and drilled it.

The ball soared toward the net. Abbas had placed it perfectly, high and to the right. Emmanuel guessed wrong and dove toward the left, totally out of position as the ball flew through the air. Then it started to curve. Dylan watched helplessly. The ball, once headed for the back of the net, spun faster and faster to the right. It brushed against the outside of the post and bounced harmlessly out of bounds.

Abbas fell to his knees. He had a horrified look on his face, as if he couldn't believe what had just happened. Dylan could tell his friend wanted the earth to open up and swallow him as Emmanuel smiled and picked up the ball.

"I said there's no way you're beating us on our field," Emmanuel said as Dylan turned and followed the ball. "You guys should just go back and play in the chicken yard."

20
Golden Goal

"I missed. I never miss." Abbas looked ready to cry.

"It's okay," said Dylan, patting his shoulder. "You'll get it next time."

Neither team came close to scoring for the rest of the half, and for the first time in the playoffs the Grandview Eagles finished regulation time in a scoreless tie. In the regular season the match would end this way, each team walking away with a point. But this was the playoffs. A tie meant ten minutes of extra time. And if the game was still even after that? Penalty shots.

"I'm sorry." Those were the first words out of Abbas's mouth as the team huddled up on the sidelines. "I should have scored. I don't know how I missed."

"Put it out of your mind," said Coach T. "Focus on the next ten minutes."

"Any one of us could have missed that shot," said Dylan. The rest of the boys nodded in agreement. Dylan knew that if he had still been playing for Regent Heights the reaction to a missed penalty kick would have been very different. Abbas would have been benched and Coach Alvarez would probably still be yelling. The team would be blaming and cursing their teammate who had made a mistake.

"You'll get another chance," said Claude. "Believe me. I have a feeling you're going to get the Golden Goal."

"Hands in," said Coach T as the referee signalled the start of extra time. "I am so proud of you, however this game ends. Now, for the last time this season, play hard, play safe, play fair. And most of all, play for each other!"

"And for the Golden Goal!" Claude grinned.

"Golden Goal!" Abbas said. "I really hope you're right."

Extra time started just as the second half had finished. Both teams played cautiously, neither wanting to make a mistake that would cost them the game. But two minutes in, Regent came close to scoring when Tony beat Mo to the ball and raced toward Grandview's goal.

Alvin rushed over to cover, forcing Tony to shoot sooner than he would have liked. It was a hard kick aimed right at Michael. It was too powerful to catch, but Michael made a great save anyway. He punched the ball to Jake who managed to clear it away from the Grandview end.

More back and forth followed, neither side getting a clear break. With less than two minutes to go it seemed certain that the game would end in penalty kicks.

But then Steven made a great clean tackle on Tony, stripping him of the ball. It rolled to Claude.

Claude had been running up and down the field all game. He must have been exhausted, but he somehow managed to gallop like a racehorse. "I love this field!" he cried out. "I could run on it all day!"

The Regent players were tired as well, and Claude's burst of energy caught them by surprise. Dylan and Abbas saw what Claude was doing and moved quickly toward Emmanuel, making sure they stayed onside.

Three defenders hurried to stop Claude. As fast as he was, there was no way he could outrun them.

"Dylan!" Claude shouted. Dribbling just enough to get some open space, Claude booted the ball toward the left touchline.

Heart racing, Dylan took the ball and ran toward the crease, ignoring the pain in his leg. A nasty bruise had spread all over his calf, but Dylan wasn't thinking about that now. The only thing on his mind was scoring on Emmanuel.

Regent had triple-teamed Claude, leaving only one defender in position. It was Tommy, and Dylan knew he was a much better player than Tommy. *I have you this time*, he thought.

Suddenly Dylan was at the top of the penalty box, only Tommy standing between himself and Emmanuel. *This ball is going in the top left corner,* Dylan thought, looking past Tommy.

Dylan cocked his leg. Tommy sprinted toward him, sliding, sticking out his foot in a desperate attempt to tackle the ball. Emmanuel bounced up and down on his feet. He stepped out of his net, cutting off the angle, ready to spring.

From the corner of his eye, Dylan saw Abbas cutting in to his right. Dylan had a high percentage shot. He wanted to score more than anything else in the world. But Abbas was wide open.

Without thinking, Dylan faked the shot. When Emmanuel dove to where he thought the ball would be, Dylan slid the ball quickly to his right. On Grandview's home field who knew what might have happened? The ball could have rolled to a stop in soft sand or it could have taken a funny bounce on a small rock. But on the smooth turf field the ball rolled perfectly to Abbas. Abbas tapped the ball into the wide open net, scoring the easiest goal of the season.

For a second there was complete silence on the field. The Regent players and fans didn't understand what had just happened. Neither did Dylan. It was only when the rest of the Grandview players swarmed Abbas, screaming and shouting in joy that Dylan realized they had done it. They had won. Grandview: 1, Regent Heights: 0. The Grandview Community School Eagles were School District champions.

Dylan was almost bowled over by Abbas running to hug him. "That was a great pass!" he said. "Thank you for believing in me. Especially after I missed the penalty shot."

"Everyone needs a little help from their friends — their true friends sometimes," Dylan replied. He was smiling so wide he thought his face would split. "Not a bad game for a bunch of losers," he added.

"No. Not bad for a bunch of losers at all," Abbas agreed.

"Golden Goal!" laughed Claude. "I said you'd score it, didn't I, Abbas? I'm never wrong when I get one of my feelings!"

On the sidelines, Dylan's mom, Mrs. Wassef and Julie were jumping up and down in excitement, hugging each other just like the boys were. Dylan saw that their eyes were wet with tears.

"I'm glad my sister was here," said Claude, looking a little teary himself. "I just wish my parents could have seen it, too. They would really have enjoyed this game."

"And my dad and brothers," said Abbas. Dylan could tell that Abbas finally felt okay talking about his past, about his family. "They would have loved this game!"

"Don't worry, Claude," said Dylan, his arms wrapped around Claude and Abbas. "You're not the only one who gets feelings, and I have a feeling your parents saw this game. So did your dad and brothers, Abbas," Dylan said. A memory of his own father's smiling face washed over him. "All of our fathers did, and they would be proud of us, I just know it."